WOODSTOK FARLEY

As the Wave Rose: Florida Tales and Other Wandering Stories

To Stan (Bingoff) Card

My best friend and co-conspirator in many of these tales. I miss you deeply, and one day I promise I'll write your story.

Tip of the Hat

surf bums looking for a brand-new high

          with the waves risin'—there is no death

(angels and demons at war)

     praying to the God of Sunday School, or Buddha,

       or Led Zeppelin

            (tryin' to save a surf bum's soul)

but how long does crazy last?

       devils with rattlesnakes

           angels in cabs

(wrong turns in Tennessee)

     permanent stay means your picture in your coffin

monsters walk among us

     darkness, midnight movies, the possibility of love

but monsters walk among us

         and the fairies aren't coming

because it takes a monster to slay a monster

     (weep for hate, let love be love)

         and the ocean accepts it all

the demons we carry inside are the real demons

       the demons we create

     and hide in swamps

until imagined angels lead us out again

but the tired world needs challenging

        or it ceases spinning in its frigid orbit

its mysteries frozen in time

        until a private dick, in brown fedora,

bourbon on his breath

looks into the case

        discovers the deepest mysteries

lie buried in the human heart

it just takes a kiss, French-style,

        to unlock them

and God and his choir of angels sing Hallelujah!

but there's more to life than a buzz & a kiss

        a dog and an old man can help you

find the truth:

look God straight in the eye

        declare that the day is amazing

        and tip your old, brown fedora

Hank Jones (2019)

Contents

I

As the Wave Rose

— choose you this day whom ye will serve —
Joshua 24:15

1

As the Wave Rose

Rutt and Dave had never seen a shark attack live before. Dave wondered if there would be a lot of blood.

"Man, all you all are messed up since that movie came out. I ain't seen it," I coughed and passed the joint to Dave, "and I ain't never gonna see—it—maaaaaannnnnn!" The smoke dragged out my last word as the mellow settled in.

I leaned back into the yellow-white sand of the dune we were perched on to watch the events as they progressed. It was now midday on the south side of the pier, and the tide was out. The three of us had wandered down the beach from the north side of the pier where the body-surfers did their thing. Everyone knew the south side was for board riders only.

We were attracted by the crowds that were assembling to watch the idiots who wanted to fish for sharks from the beach. A whale had beached itself sometime in the night, and during high tide, the sharks had been feasting on its carcass. Sharks were circling the area, but they couldn't get to the whale.

Meanwhile, the board-riders waited for those fishing to clear out so they could catch some waves—they simply ignored the sharks. From up the beach came this hulk-like man with a surf rod. Rutt coughed out smoke along with a laugh as this obvious new shore-fisher tried to get his bait out; the waves kept washing it back to shore.

"You know, I bet that idiot will try to swim his bait out over the waves," I offered with eyes half-closed from the weed.

At about that time, Hulk-man grabbed his bait and started swimming out past the reef.

"See, told ya."

"Bet a two-finger lid he don't make it back to shore," Rutt said with a devilish smile.

"Do you think we should tell him a shark has his scent?" Dave asked as he pointed at the large shadow on the reef, and then he took another toke. He held the smoke as long as he could before snorting half of it out through his nose and then giving up with a cough.

I decided to give Hulk-man an opportunity to make it to shore and started yelling at the onlookers down at the surf's edge, while pointing.

"Hey, shark! Get that dude outta there!"

Wind and waves created too much noise for anyone to hear me from our sand dune perch. Dave and Rutt joined in shouting, and finally we got someone who saw the dorsal fin moving parallel down the reef while Hulk-man was walking waist-deep in the surf back to shore. At the last minute, he finally heard the shouting and turned to see the shadow moving lazily toward him; he then attempted to run through the surf—if one could call it running. Imagine one running through concrete that is almost set. It was kinda comical. Fortunately for him, the shark turned and headed out for the bait that was floating beyond the waves.

Much to our surprise, the Hulk-man made it back to his rod lying on the beach and dug his heels into the sand just as the shark grabbed the bait.

He caught it! It was a nine-foot white-tip.

"Man, that was freaky! Looks like I owe you some weed," Rutt said.

"Yeah you do and none of that Gainesville Green shit! I smoked a whole five-finger lid and didn't even get a buzz. I even tried soaking it with Listerine and burying it for a couple of weeks and still nothin'.'"

"That's 'cause you smoke too much. You got to lay off the weed for at least a couple of hours a day to get your system right. You stay stoned way too much," Dave declared with the giggle of a doper who smoked way too much.

"I hear there's a party at the shell-pits tonight," said Rutt. "Anyone wanna go?"

Turning and walking backward facing us, Dave offered, "Hey, why don't we head up to Blowin' Rock and see if Reefer's surfin' tonight. It's a full moon, and you know how he digs a full moon, man."

Now this Reefer is somewhat of a local legend in the surfing community here. Folks say that he only surfs at night during a full moon. That's what folks say.

No one knows much about him, only that he lives on a houseboat in the swamp and settled there after coming home from 'Nam. Folks believe he's a demon of sorts. They say he don't fear death because he's already dead. I believe it since nobody who surfs at night could possibly be human. Most of what folks say about Reefer probably has its origins from late night campfires on the beach when some hapless tourists are present, and the surfers are feeling their beer. But the simple truth is—the dude surfs like a demon without fear, and he surfs at *night*!

"You ever been to his place in the swamp? Those that's been there say you don't come back," Rutt whispered.

"Now think about it, man. How can you tell someone that you don't come back if you don't come back?" I offered.

Rutt and Dave both thought about it for a minute. Rutt finally understood, but Dave's mind drifted off into the fog of stoned.

"Hey, man. What'd ya say we go check out Reefer's houseboat and see if there are any graves," Dave offered from the fog.

And Dave thinks I smoke too much.

"Dave, the dude lives in a swamp! There ain't no graves. There ain't no dirt to dig in. All you gotta do is throw someone in the water, and the 'gators will do the rest."

"Still, wouldn't it be far-out to go there and see if he's sacrificing some virgin to the surf gods," Dave offered getting excited about the possibilities of the evening's entertainment involving naked virgins and blood. I think the lack of blood with the shark earlier disappointed him. So, we all agreed to meet later when the sun set and head out to the point on the Loxahatchee River where Reefer docked his houseboat.

Now it's one thing to go to the river in the daytime, but at night it gets really spooky. Folks who don't know the swamp don't realize how dark it can be. In the darkness, everything runs together—the sky, the trees, the water. It's hard to tell where one ends, and the other begins. If you live on the river, you do so because you like your privacy, and you don't need any security—the swamp and the things in the swamp are your security.

We stared in the direction where we believed Reefer's boat was docked, but we couldn't see any evidence that it was in front of us since the moon had not yet come up. Darkness worked its magic and produced a chill that only I seemed to feel. The only light at the moment came from the red glow of the joint as it was passed around.

"Man! Where'd you get this shit? This stuff is amazing!" Rutt said as he tried to hold it in, but coughed out through his nose. "Damn, that's good shit!"

"I scored it from some freak who said he brought it back from 'Nam. Said he smuggled a whole key. Sells three-finger lids for fifty bucks," I replied with some pride as I took the joint from Rutt.

"Man, I'd pay a hundred and fifty for this shit. It's so good that I'm seein' colored lights," Dave remarked as he pointed toward the river's edge.

But it wasn't the pot that was making the lights; they were coming from the boat in front of us—Reefer's boat. The lights varied like the colors of the rainbow. They were red, they were blue, they were green, and then they were yellow. The lights were bright and then faded to an afterglow like the flash leftover from a camera's bulb. Rutt pointed at the shadow walking through the lights. Somebody was home.

"Let's get out of here," Dave whispered. "That dude is conjurin' some spell, and I don't want to be a flea again."

"A flea!" I said a little too loud and then lowered my voice, "Man, you must have been trippin' on some heavy shit! When were you ever a flea?"

Before Dave could remember an answer, the door of the houseboat shut loud in the dark stillness of the swamp. Reefer walked quietly down the dock right toward where we were standing and stopped in front of us. His voice was a little above the swamp noises of cricket chirps, frog bellows, and mullet slaps on the water.

"What in the hell do you guys want?" Reefer muttered, annoyed.

Dave pushed past us with a shaking, extended hand and with an overly excited voice said, "Reefer! What's happenin'? Hey, we were headin' out to Blowin' Rock and wondered if you were going to be there? It's a full moon and all, and we know how much you dig that." Then Dave offered Reefer a hit from the joint he was holding, but Reefer simply shook his head and walked around us to his VW bus.

Dave blew out a big sigh of relief when he realized that Reefer wasn't going to turn him into an insect and nervously muttered, "Let's split." And before I could react Dave and Rutt had jumped in the Falcon and were headed down the sugar-sand road without me. I wondered how far they would get before they realized I wasn't with them. I was pretty sure they wouldn't turn around.

"Looks like your friends left you behind," Reefer grumbled as he turned to face me.

At this moment the music of the swamp got really loud. My head began to spin as the noise and the fear of standing so close to Reefer and not knowing if he would turn me into something settled into my brain. It didn't help that the mellow fog in my head began to slip into the paranoid muddle in my stomach. The only response I could come up with was a terrified "Are you really dead, or did you make some kinda pact with the devil?"

Amused by the myth which seemed familiar to him, Reefer leaned close to my face and smiled as he whispered with a growl, "What do you think?"

The full-blown paranoia was now coming from a completely scared-straight head. I knew any minute that this dude was about to cast some torturous spell on me and throw me to the swamp, never to be heard from again. All I could come up with was "I once dated a Satanist," hoping to appease his demon spirit. Reefer leaned back with a puzzled look as he narrowed his eyes and carefully studied my face to determine my seriousness.

He dropped his shoulders and looked downward to the ground and then looked up into the darkness as he softly said, "I ain't no demon." Then looking back at me with a glare he snarled, "Man, where do you idiots come up with this stuff. Why would you even think such a thing," he asked, but this time with a kinda sadness.

"The lights! We saw colored lights coming from your boat, man. We figured you were casting a spell."

Turning his head back to the boat to see from our perspective, he simply said, "TV, man, TV," but something in his voice didn't convince me that we saw TV lights.

Slowly and without clear reason, the paranoia left, and the darkness of the swamp and all its sounds did not seem so frightening. I felt a peacefulness near Reefer that no weed could induce. Shoving my hands into my baggies and relaxing my shoulders I asked without hesitation,

"Well, if you ain't no demon and you ain't dead or nuthin', then why do you surf at night? No one can surf like you do and still be human, man."

This question amused him. He turned his head back toward me and gently smiling, he asked, "Why do you surf, man?"

Now of all the questions Reefer could have asked me this was the most profound. Surfers, I mean real down-to-the-core surfers, whether they ride a board or not, do not answer with a simple "because it's fun!" No, real surfers have a passion, a connection with the sea that's not that easy to explain. It's felt by other surfers, so explaining it does not always take words. To those who don't surf, it's hard to describe, but I knew Reefer would understand.

"When I'm in the water, I taste its saltiness, and I feel it cradling me, supporting me. Then as the wave begins to build, I feel the pull. It's as if there's this mighty force of nature that can't be controlled, yet somehow nature allows me to share in that power. It's a high that can't be duplicated, just revisited each time, brand new, over and over with each wave. It's heaven, man!"

"Exactly!" Reefer shouted as he looked to the heavens and nodded with that brotherhood of understanding that all riders of the waves acknowledge. "It's heaven," he said with less enthusiasm and almost as if there was some regret that had worked its way into his very soul.

Pondering this I braved my next question: "Reefer, did the war get you all tortured up? Right now, you seem like someone who's invitin' danger by surfin' the way you do. You got some kind of death wish or somethin'?"

I truly seemed to touched a nerve with Reefer; he did not answer immediately, but then with a grave whisper, "It was a war, but not 'Nam. It was a war that was before your time. A war that I walked away from just because of that pull of the wave."

Now I don't know a lot, but one thing I know is that Reefer wasn't old enough for World War II or even Korea. What war could he be talking about? Reefer did not let me ask as he moved back toward his bus and began to check the lashings on his boards. Then turning to me, he asked, "wanna come along?"

Driving to Blowin' Rock should have been the most amazing buzz I could have ever experienced. Here I was with the god of surfing going to witness man's ultimate test—surfing at night as the moon was rising—and yet I couldn't utter a word. It felt like a solemn occasion, like a funeral. Reefer looked straight ahead and offered no conversation initially. Finally, he broke the silence by asking a question that was more like a statement that didn't require an answer.

"Did you ever consider that death is a myth? Something made up to satisfy not seeing the other side. That it's not a stopping point. Did you ever think that you simply move from one reality to another, accepting the consequences that come with each new reality?"

Then he went silent again.

Looking at him in the glow of the dash lights, I knew that I was not seasoned enough in life to answer with any profound thought. The years spent stoning my brain had put such thoughts on hold. The answer to Reefer's question belonged to the ones who had faced death and somehow put it off for the moment. Here was a man who faced death every time he entered the water, and he was about to do it again.

As we parked and unloaded his boards, Reefer maintained his silence; his eyes were on something in the water that I could not see. I was not sure if it was some zone he was in or if it was something that transcended the moment. Perhaps he was pondering his own question.

I sat down on a dune and watched as Reefer pushed off into the dark water, bobbing leisurely over the waves. When he reached the place where the bigger waves started to build, he faced into them rather than turning toward the shore while straddling his board. I could make out his outline in the light of the rising moon, and I noticed that he had his hands raised as if in the worship of the wave gods. It was at that moment, something unnatural began to occur. I noticed that the moon, which was now fully visible over the horizon, was starting to disappear. My first thought was a freighter was slowly moving in front of the moon's light, but as I looked more intently, I realized it was a wave rising in front of it. Rising rapidly, it dwarfed Reefer as he continued his worship. It made me think for a moment that Reefer was offering himself up to it without any objections. He fully acknowledged and accepted the consequences of this reality and expected the next reality to also belong to his choice. Here was no ordinary man. Reefer was not a man who was inhabited by demons, as many believed, but driven by something much bigger, something much greater.

By this time the moon was completely blocked by the wave as Reefer slowly turned his board into it. There was no doubt I was witnessing something extraordinary that few, if any, had ever seen, and Reefer allowed me to be a part of this moment. He allowed me to be a part of the pull — as the wave rose.

2

The River Is a Dark Lady

The river is a dark lady. Black. Mysterious. Unhurried. Tranquil. This river has worked her fingers into my very soul. Growing up on her shores—I swam naked in her darkness, I drank from her bottomless depths, I labored over fallen giant cypresses to her headwaters and, yet, I still lusted for her anew each time I came upon her again and again and again.

The moon oft wills me to explore her curves, to glide up and down her tributaries, to run my fingers through her mossy hair that dangles along her shore, to navigate her silently as her night sounds moan and sing while her body rises and falls along with the tides.

The sun too beckons me to ride the river, but in a more thrilling way. We are exposed for all the world to see, as we move along together with the help of both metal and wood. The sun warms my passion; it stirs my longings for new ways to become one, one with this beautiful, dark lady.

As I stare up river, the sun comes closer and closer and closer. It enters and settles into the front of my canoe and extends a warm hand toward me. Slowly the hand begins to drip golden droplets onto the floor of the canoe as the glowing orb gradually melts into a puddle upon the bow seat. The golden *droplets spill over the side of the canoe becoming a golden liquid spreading out over the river's surface, beading upon that surface like oil upon . . . .*

"HEY, FARTFACE! You gonna paddle back there or let me do all the work," yelled Dave over his shoulder.

"Let him be, man. He's peakin'!" Rutt said as he sat low in the middle of the canoe trailing his right hand, fingers spread wide in the surface's warm, dark-colored water.

The Loxahatchee River appears dark when it runs deep, but actually, it's tea-like in color from the tannin exposure. Groundwater in South Florida has always been that way and causes folks with shallow wells to cuss on laundry day.

"Hey, look!" Dave said, pointing to the canoe across the river. "Tourists!"

You can always tell tourists: they're bright pink because they take the sunshine all in one dose. They come in hordes from the north and spoil the leisurely pace of our state and then they beat it back to wherever they temporarily migrated from to tell lies about the publically-indecent bikini or the dark-tanned surf bum that got away.

"Let's freak 'em out," I said as I ruddered my paddle to bring us within earshot.

The tourists had happened upon a gator swimming to the left of the bow of their rented Jonathan Dickson State Park canoe. Tourists often freak out seeing nature moving effortlessly through the still, dark water. The gator wasn't that old, only about five feet from snout to tail. When they are bothered, they'll simply slip beneath the surface only to resurface at some distant point later. We all knew this, and so our customary tourist tease began.

"Nice gator," I yelled, cupping my hands to my mouth, forcing the sound over the water.

"You're alright as long as she doesn't go under," yelled Rutt.

And then without another word we paddled on, heading downriver while the gator went under.

"HEYYYY! What'll we do?" they yelled, grabbing the gunwales thinking that if they held on tightly, they wouldn't tip over.

Of course, in their fear, they offset the balance of the canoe and came dangerously close to joining the often elusive reptile. The more they tried to balance the rocking, the more the canoe resisted. It took them several minutes to settle the movement from their panic weight shift, but still, they held tightly to the canoe's sides drifting into the mangrove shoreline whose long-fingered roots beckoned them to come and tangle themselves up in the Spanish moss and red bugs.

Looking back, I saw the gator surface as I expected further up the river and out of the notice of the ignorant sun-gluttons. Laughing, I corrected our course toward the opposite shore disregarding their fading pleas.

"Man, I never get tired of spookin' tourists. Reckon they'll be stuck in the mangroves till some cotton-mouth chases them back out into the river," smiled Rutt.

Pulling the canoe up on shore, Dave grunted a reply, "Who cares man. That's three down and a million to go. I hate tourists."

"What's eating Dave?" I asked Rutt while throwing the life-jackets on to the grass to dry in the sun.

"I don't know, man. He's been freakin' out ever since he did that Orange Sunshine last night. It usually don't last this long, but he's still trippin' as far as I can tell. You ate some. Are you freakin' out, or is it just Dave?"

"I think it's just Dave. I feel fantastic! You should of seen the sun melting onto the bow a moment ago."

Dave came ambling over and threw a baggie at Rutt. "Twist one up will ya? I'm goin' for a dip."

He steadied himself on the roots of a mangrove, holding onto a branch above. Something came loose from the branch and wiggled down his arm. Looking surprised, he grabbed the snake and threw it into the dark water and then dove in after.

When he surfaced, I asked with a smile, "Hey, Dave, did you get a good look at what kind of snake that was?"

Twisting his head in the water in an effort to locate the serpent, Dave took a few strokes and was back onshore.

"Shit, man! I didn't even think to look. I just dove in. Reckon' it was a moccasin?"

"Moccasins don't hang out in trees," chuckled Rutt as he sat cross-legged on the sand rolling a fat doobie. Looking up at Dave with a grin, he said, "At least, I don't think they do," and then looking at me he winked.

Grabbing a life-jacket to use as a pillow, Dave laid down on the sugar-sand shoreline and reached for the joint. Taking a deep drag and holding it in his lungs as long as he could, he passed it on. As he slowly let out the smoke, he dreamily looked up at the clear blue afternoon with its sporadic clouds.

"Did you guys know that the Commies have figured out how to seed the clouds with LSD to create acid rain so that everyone will be trippin' when they take over the world?"

"Dave, I don't think that acid rain is a Communistic conspiracy. . . ."

"Hey, anyone want to paddle up to Trap's? It's been a while since we been there. Maybe we can find his gold this time."

Now Trapper Nelson is a local legend of sorts to the folks who have grown up around the river. He was known as the *Tarzan of the Loxahatchee* during his peak years in the 40s and 50s with his tourist-attracting zoo on the banks of the river. He had low pens of restless wild boars, tall cages of curious raccoons, and elegant pink flamingos wandering freely in along the shore. There was even had an old chimpanzee chained to a dead cypress. They found Trapper dead in

'68 from a gunshot wound to the head. It was labeled a suicide, but most locals didn't buy it. When authorities searched his cabin, they found over five-thousand Mexican gold coins stuffed in his chimney. Legend says there's more buried somewhere on his land, now owned by the state park.

"Count me in," I said as I ran and snatched the lifejacket from under Dave's head causing him to jump up and chase me into the river.

"And maybe Big Bertha will be out sunning," Dave said as he pushed me under the water and then ran toward the canoe laughing, no longer in a funk.

We climbed into the canoe and headed back upriver, all talking about Trap's lost treasure. Looking to the far bank for the tourists, I noticed the canoe was empty and floating back downriver to turn itself in. They must have tried to escape through the mangroves. Bad idea for the tourists. Good idea for a hungry swamp.

As we neared the bend that led to Trap's place, we slowed up to navigate the cut cypress trees that he felled in the river. When Trapper Nelson decided he'd had enough of society—largely due to the paranoia he had against the government—he cut the massive trees and let them serve as an obstacle to anyone who wanted to come to his part of the river. Boats often ripped their fiberglass hulls on the trees just below the dark water surface. The only ones getting through nowadays were those who travel by canoe.

Just like we expected, Big Bertha was sunning herself on the bank opposite Trap's docks. Big Bertha is an eleven-foot gator that has been hanging around Trap's place since any of us could remember. The story is that Trapper raised her from an egg, and together they put on many a show for the tourists. After Trap was found dead, Bertha took up residence across the river from his place, and some believe she is waiting for him to return.

Paddling up to the dock, I noticed that the deterioration of his zoo pens and cabins appeared to be due more to vandalism than what weathering time can bring. Probably some idiot tourists. No self-respecting, native-born Floridian would dare destroy what had been revered for so many years. Trap's self-imposed exile represented man's rebellion against an oppressive government—a sort of modern-day revolutionary war hero. No one but outsiders would demolish and desecrate this hallowed ground. Sure, we dig around and look under things, but we always put it back the way we found it. Stepping ashore we noticed doors were pulled off hinges, furniture was broken, fences to the holding pens were pushed over, and there were holes dug everywhere.

"Man, someone freaked on Trapper's place," Rutt said, shaking his head in disgust. Dave, surveying the damage, wondered out loud, "I reckon' they were looking for Trap's gold."

Saddened by the unexpected destruction, I ambled over to Trap's cabin and stopped short when I noticed someone or something was moving inside. Quickly turning to signal the others while leaving my back to the door proved to be a mistake. A strong, salt-weathered hand reached out from the dark doorway and grabbed my shoulder.

"HOLY SHIT." I yelled as I tried to run, but the hand held tight and firm. When I turned to see what was keeping me from getting away, it took a moment for my brain to register what my eyes were seeing.

"Reefer! Reefer, you scared the hell out of me! What are you doing here?"

Slowly putting his finger to his lips, Reefer locked eyes with each one of us. The tall, ocean-muscled figure didn't have to say it twice. No one, I mean, no one argued with Reefer. There was something about this tanned and mysterious surfer that scared most, especially Dave. But Dave's nervousness around Reefer usually brought out some comment Dave had not carefully thought through.

"Say, Reefer, I didn't know you came out in the daylight. What you doin' at Trap's? Ain't no waves on the river. You . . ."

Reefer's angry eyes brought Dave to silence. Reefer never discouraged Dave's paranoia. I think Reefer was actually amused at some of the rumors that found their way to him. It provided the privacy he seems to cherish.

Motioning us into Trap's cabin, Reefer looked around the other buildings as if he knew someone or something was hiding in the shadows.

Quietly, Reefer told us about some Mexican *banditos* that were here looking for Trap's gold. He quickly filled us in that Trap had stolen their gold years ago while in Mexico. It seems that he spent some time in prison there and learned about a stash of gold coins in some Pachuca hideaway. He relieved them of that gold, and they wanted it back. They had tracked him here because of a newspaper article written about the suspiciousness of his death and the discovery of the five-thousand gold coins.

How Reefer knew all this, I wasn't sure, but I figured I'd ask later. Right now, me and the boys just wanted to get back down the river as fast as we could. Reefer indicated that that was not too good an idea at the moment since the *banditos* were still in the area. He said we needed to wait until dark. Now navigating the river at night normally is not difficult when the moon is full, but the moon was due late tonight, and with a dark river, it would not be so easy. And there were still the felled cypresses to deal with. It wasn't going to go quickly. Besides, there are places on the river that are quite narrow, and I didn't like the idea of what could be hiding onshore. Someone or something could do us harm, and no one would ever know. Reefer might be able to wait till dark, but me and the boys needed to get to those canoes, and we needed to do it now! Reefer seemed to sense my mental plotting and fixing his eyes on mine, he slowly shook his head from left to right.

Forgetting the need to whisper as well as his fear of Reefer, Dave argued, "So, if they're here looking for gold, that means there is gold! We just gotta look where they haven't looked," and he started for the door.

Pulling Dave back into the cabin's darkness, Reefer spoke in hushed, firm tones only a breath away from Dave's face, "Not a smart move there, Sherlock. Those guys mean business, and they can just as easily bury you in one of those holes they've already dug. You understand!"

Letting go of Dave and softening he spoke to all of us, "Again, I think it's better we wait till dark," and looking at each one of us he asked, "everyone agree?"

Dave returned to pacing the other side of the cabin, and I decided to wrestle with some of my fear as well, "Say, Reefer, why are you here? Just how do you know all this stuff about Trap and these other guys? And, by the way, I've never seen you this far inland before and, in the daylight, too. What's the deal?"

I kept my questions quiet not only because of the danger outside but because Dave is not the only one intimidated by Reefer. No one knows anything about him. All we know is that he only surfs at night and only surfs during a full moon. Nobody in their right mind surfs at night. Nobody. For a moment, I thought Dave was right. Maybe Reefer is something other than natural. For example, just how in the world did he get to Trap's? There wasn't another canoe tied up at the docks. Maybe he didn't come by river. Maybe he came in his VW bus by the state park road. Maybe he came with the *banditos*. The *banditos*! Maybe he was somehow involved with the *banditos*?

Reefer's eyes narrowed, looking intently into mine as he stepped closer to me. My fear began to return with a violence shaking me as I watched him slowly raise his hand to my shoulder and then point a finger outside hissing, "Ssshh." We all heard voices. From Reefer's expression, I guessed these weren't park rangers coming to the rescue. Turning slowly in the cabin's darkness, I saw the voices carried guns in shoulder holsters, and some had shotguns. There were four that I could see, and Reefer indicated by pointing to the one with the big straw hat as he whispered, "That's the leader."

One of them carrying a shotgun shouted excitedly, "*Hermanos*, look," pointing at the canoe, "this was not here when we came."

Without being told, they quickly began to spread out searching each building.

Reefer shoved us through the cabin's back window, and we made a beeline to the palmetto thickets and sawgrass. Dave cussed out loud when he tripped and fell face-first into the sugar sand. The chase was on.

If you happen to grow up in and around swamps, you can usually navigate their difficulty. This gave us an advantage. We've been playing in the swamps since we were kids. Those giving chase weren't fairing so well. Sawgrass can cut you to ribbons if you don't respect it. Now either Reefer had not come out of the cabin, or he was heading in another direction because when we stopped to catch our breath, it was just me, Rutt, and Dave with the noisy *banditos* in painful pursuit.

We decided to lead these novices deeper into the swamp and then circle around and follow the river back to the canoe. It was tourist teasing for the second time today. We kept moving deeper and deeper into the sawgrass all the while using their Spanglish curses to guage our distance from them. When we felt that we had sufficient space between them and Trap's, we began a wide circle back to the river and then followed it back to the canoe. When we got back, we noticed that the one with the big straw hat was keeping vigil over our canoe. Crouching down behind some palmetto, Rutt whispered that we needed a diversion—something to draw Straw-hat guy away from the canoe.

From out of nowhere, Reefer came running straight at the dude! Surprised and panicking, the man fired both barrels from his shotgun directly into Reefer's chest, but the big surfer's forward momentum carried him into his assailant, and somehow he managed to roll both of them into the river. Without a sound, the river pulled them down into her darkness.

Big Bertha eased her massive body beneath the dark waters as well.

It took us a moment to shake off the shock of what we had just witnessed when Rutt brought Dave and me back to reality. "Let's get the hell out of here!" he yelled, running for the canoe.

"What about Reefer," I mumbled as my eyes scanned the river for some movement under the surface. But none came. Quickly pushing off, I turned and kept my eyes searching the river for any reason to turn around.

None came.

After letting park rangers know just enough to keep us out of the immediate investigation, we sent them to Trap's to check on some vandals who were digging up the place.

"Man, I can't believe Reefer's gone," Rutt said.

"Yeah, man, it's a bummer. I really dug the guy," Dave said while staring off into the night sky.

Turning to Dave with an expression of surprise, Rutt exclaimed, "What! Man, you always said Reefer freaked you out. You was always worried about what he was gonna turn you into. Truth is I figured you'd be relieved to see him gone."

"Just 'cause the dude freaked me out doesn't mean that I didn't have respect for his surfin'. Man, ain't no one can take that away from him. Not no one. Not even me. Yeah, the dude made me nervous, but I did respect his way with a wave. I did respect that. That's the truth!"

"Man, we're all gonna miss Reefer. He was one of a kind. He had all our respect. There was always somethin' weird about him, or, I don't know, maybe more mysterious than weird, I guess. The dude was definitely hiding something about his past. Now we'll never know. His secrets are buried at the bottom of the Loxahatchee and protected by Big Bertha," I said, choking back surprised emotion.

Rutt and Dave decided to split for Blowin' Rock saying they wanted to be around familiar Reefer territory. Maybe familiarity would ease the sadness of losing the only real hero our surfing community had. As they drove off, a full moon began to rise.

Me, I headed out to Reefer's houseboat. I needed familiarity as well, but I wanted to be alone. I didn't know what to do now that Reefer was gone. I was just beginning to know this dark character and his suicidal ways with a surfboard. I had been certain if I stayed around him long enough, he might let me inside his head.

That was probably more wishful thinking on my part. The night he let me tag along and watch him surf in the moonlight was not an invitation to the life-long buddies' club. He told me that night he had been in a war, but never said what war or what it had done to him. I was sure something in his past haunted him—I'd never know now. What I did know was Reefer gave his life to save ours. Not so sure I could have done that; in fact, I'm quite sure I don't have that in me. Maybe Reefer could have taught me how it is possible, but now . . . now all the answers lay at the bottom of that dark river.

Pulling up to Reefer's dock, I noticed there was a light on in his boat, and his bus was parked out front. My first thought was maybe the police brought it back and were searching his place, but then I remembered we hadn't told them about Reefer and Straw-hat guy. Suddenly from out of nowhere, paranoia began to work its way into my brain, and I quietly eased my Beetle into reverse and began turning away back down the sugar-sand road. Looking in my rear-view mirror, I saw someone step out from the boat carrying a surfboard.

In the full moon, I saw . . . Reefer!

3

The Waves Just Aren't Big Enough Anymore

Pizza crusts! Thirty damn pizza crusts! What the hell am I gonna do with thirty damn pizza crusts? If I hadn't been cutting through the alley trying to beat the storm, if Whaletail hadn't spotted me through the open half-door of the pizza shack, if she hadn't asked if I wanted anything—anything at all—then I wouldn't be trying to stuff thirty damn pizza crusts into a Frigidaire fifteen-crust only freezer box.

The rain was coming down in sheets now, and a knock at the door made me wonder if Whaletail had cut her shift short. It was certain she wasn't coming by for pizza. Looking out through the jalousie windows, I saw two long-hairs standing in the pouring rain. Opening the door, I realized one of the long-hairs was a skinny girl. In the dark, she looked just like a guy.

"Hey man, Strummer said that we might crash here tonight. They call me Banty, you know like the rooster. This here's Patti," he said, tilting his head in the direction of the girl who was looking mighty paranoid. "You Fartface?"

"I go by MJ," I declared, perturbed by the nickname the town had given me. "Doesn't anybody go by their given names around here?"

"Patti does 'cause she ain't from 'round here. Nicknames are part of this town for as long as I can remember. Everybody gets one. It's like a rite of passage, once you get yours you know you are a part of the town forever," said Banty as they both stepped in. I left them dripping at the door, soaked to the bone, and went to the bathroom to fetch some towels. Only then did I remember about the pot plants hanging upside down to dry on the towel racks. There were newspapers on the floor to catch any runs of sap. After handing them the towels, I figured they wouldn't narc on me, so I told Patti that the bathroom was that way, don't mind the crop, and watch out for the sticky newspapers. She never once looked me in the eye, nor did she smile, she just looked at Banty for reassurance before disappearing into the bath. "Sit down, man. You cain't hurt that couch. You said Strummer sent ya. How long you been knowin' Strummer?"

"I grew up here. Been away for some time. Me and Patti were cutting through town when the storm hit. Ran into Strummer over at Sugarland Auditorium, and he said that folks sometimes crash here. We just need a place for the night, or at least till the storm passes. Is it cool?"

"Sure man. Hey, you guys want a pizza?"

Patti emerged from the bathroom with the same paranoid eyes and froze when someone suddenly started banging on the door. It sounded like they were using their whole forearm against the wood, shouting, "Open up! It's the cops!" Banty freaked and grabbed Patti heading for the bedroom just as the front door flew open. Strummer came falling through, laughing so hard he could barely stand. Hearing the laughter, Banty and Patti came back to the living room and Banty angrily yelled at Strummer, "That ain't funny, you butthole! You about made me crap my pants," but slowly he began to smile at the joke and then was laughing along with Strummer. Patti kept her paranoid expression.

"Man," Strummer said pointing at Banty with tears in his eyes, "I never seen someone move so fast. Got somethin' to hide there, Banty?" he said with a smirk. Then, while locking eyes with me, Strummer tilted his head slightly toward Banty and mouthed something silently I couldn't understand, but left me feeling uneasy.

In the darkness beyond the doorway, someone stood holding an umbrella; it was Batman, the town drunk. At one time Batman was a commercial airline pilot, but after inheriting a large sum of money, he decided to devote himself to drink and never flew again. Batman was older than any of us and came from a prominent sugarcane family. He's the only one in this town who would even think of using an umbrella in the rain.

Changing the subject, Banty asked, "Hey, Fartface, mind if me and Patti take a shower and get out of these wet clothes?"

Looking back at Banty with a new nervousness I said, "Sure, man. And it's MJ! I'll get you some dry things and put a couple of pizzas in."

While I was grabbing some T-shirts and shorts, Strummer stepped into the bedroom. In a whisper, he said, "While we were packing up at the auditorium the fuzz came by. I thought they were gonna complain about the music, but they just asked if we'd seen any strangers tonight. Said a truck driver was killed and robbed just outside of town and two long-hairs were seen runnin' from the truck. Right after they left, Banty and Patti showed up." Looking back through the bedroom door to see if anyone was listening, Strummer continued, "I figure that in the dark two long-hairs could be one long-hair and a skinny chick. Banty and his ol' lady were mighty paranoid when they showed up tonight. Just thought I'd warn ya."

"Thanks, Strummer," I said as I drew a deep breath. "I knew somethin' wasn't right with them two. Now I got to figure a way to get rid of 'em. Any ideas?"

"No, but I'm sorry, man. I didn't put it all together before I told them about crashin' here. Guess seeins' how it's my fault they ended up here, I'll hang around and do what I can to help."

"'Preciate it. Guess I better go make some pizzas. Hey, guess what Whaletail gave me?"

As the oven was warming up, I stuck my head in the fridge to find something to put on the pizzas. Stepping out of the bath and rubbing his hair with a towel, Banty commented. "Nice crop of weed in there," pointing back with his thumb. "You planning on selling any, 'cause I sure could use some. Came upon some bread awhile back, so I could pay you for it."

Strummer and I looked at one another and Banty noticed the exchange. All of a sudden, I noticed Batman was still standing outside in the rain holding his umbrella. Batman was too polite to walk in without an invitation.

"You just gonna stand there in the rain or you comin' in Batman?" I said teasingly.

He shook off the umbrella and stepped inside as I continued teasing, "Where the hell you get an umbrella? Somebody leave it at the bar?"

Batman mumbled something no one understood. No one ever understands Batman unless he's sober and that only happens when he wakes up on Sunday morning just before 10 am. He has some kinda arrangement with the owners of the liquor store who sell to him from the drive-thru; everyone else has to wait for their Sunday beer till the Baptists get out of church at noon.

We ate our pizza and smoked a few, then everyone crashed. I gave Banty and Patti the bedroom. When the sun came shining through the jalousies, I rolled off the couch and noticed Batman sitting straight up and very proper in the recliner with his hair combed back and holding the umbrella with one hand between his knees. He asked in a very proper Southern voice, "Would you be so kind as to drive me to Pack's liquor store?"

It must be 10 am Sunday!

After dropping Batman off, I decided a road trip to the coast to see Reefer was in order.

I'd been inland far too long, and I needed to ride some waves. I stopped by the house to see if Strummer wanted to go, but he said he had rehearsal and that Banty and Patti had left before he got up. I went to grab some pot from the bath, and that's when I realized Banty had helped himself to some of my crop. Even though there was a hundred dollars in twenties on the bathroom counter, Banty had taken more than a hundred dollars' worth. It pissed me off, and Strummer said it was just like Banty. Said he never was any good. So, I grabbed some weed and stuffed it in my cut-offs and after lashing my boards to the top of the green super Beetle with driftwood bumpers, I headed east. The clouds were gathering—another storm was coming!

Once the buzz settled into a cruise, I turned the 8-track up and rolled down the windows. While Skynyrd was cranking out a triple lead, up ahead I saw this skinny chick thumbing and before the brain fog cleared, Patti was climbing in the back while Banty was climbing in the front. Pointing a gun at me, he told me to drive.

"Man, Banty this ain't cool! First, you take my plants, then you stick a gun in my face. I even let you crash at my place, and this is how you pay me back. This ain't cool, man! This just ain't cool!"

"I left some bread, man," he said almost apologetically. Turning toward the window, he lowered the gun between his legs.

Hesitating before I asked, and looking straight ahead, I blurted out, "You killed that truck driver, didn't ya?"

Banty turned toward me, and his expression darkened, "That little shit had it coming. He was hitting on my ol' lady while I was crashing in his sleeper. Nobody touches my ol' lady. Nobody! Now I hate this, 'cause you're a decent head, but I can't have you goin' to the pigs." Pointing the gun at the side of my head, he ordered me to pull over.

The first few big drops fell from the sky as I slowed the Beetle down and moved to the side of the road. My buzz made everything seem so surreal and kept me from freaking out. Silently, I prayed to anyone or anything that might get me out of this. I prayed to the God of Sunday School, to Buddha, and even to Led Zeppelin. I mean, after all, they had that Stairway song and the *Houses of the Holy* album; figured they must have some sort of connection to a higher power. Maybe, whatever's out there, if they're listening, could strike Banty with lightning or something cool like that.

"Come on, get out," Banty ordered waving the gun in my face.

Looking at the storm clouds above, I found myself praying again. *Please, anybody? I'm really in a bad way and could use some help now! Please!* Suddenly, someone pushed me to the ground. I could hear what sounded like body punches and groans coming from a struggle behind me, but I was too afraid to look up. Then it got really quiet, and a strong hand grabbed me by the shirt, lifting me without any effort. Then strong hands turned me around, and I found myself face to face with Reefer.

"Reefer, where the hell did you come from? Man, what happened to Banty?" I said as I noticed he was lying face down in the grass and not responding to Patti's pleas to wake up. "Did ya kill him?"

"He ain't dead, just unconscious. Let's get out of here before he comes to."

"You just gonna leave him here?"

"What do you want to do, give them a lift to the bus station? He killed that truck driver and just now tried to kill you. Let's just get out of here now!" Reefer said angrily as he stepped into the passenger's side of the Beetle and closed the door.

Then came the hard rain.

I drove for some time before I finally asked Reefer how he came to be at that place at that exact moment. His VW bus was nowhere around.

Looking out the window and without turning to me, he said, "You asked for some help. I was the help."

"What do you mean, I asked you for help? I prayed for some help. You tellin' me you're the answer to my prayer?"

Turning to me, he said with all seriousness, "Yeah, I'm the answer to your prayer."

"I don't understand. What the hell you talkin' about?"

Turning back to the window, he said heavily, "I overheard your prayer, so I came."

"What do you mean overheard my prayer? What—are you tellin' me you're psychic or somethin'?"

"No, I ain't psychic," he said with heaviness in his voice. Then looking at me and appearing to study my face, he continued, "I'm what you created humans call . . . an angel. A created being, but not human."

"What the hell you mean 'angel'? You mean like with wings and halos and glowin' in the dark shit?"

"We don't have wings. That's something you humans made up. Look, I know that this is hard to wrap your head around.

"Remember when I told you I was in a war? Well, I was in a *war*. It was a war back before humans. A war in the Creator's relm. A war in what you call heaven," Reefer said with a heavy sigh and then he turned back to the window and looked up into the dark rain clouds.

He stared as if he were seeing something that was beyond them, something I couldn't see.

Pulling the car over to the side of the road, I shut off the engine and looked at Reefer, thinking surely any minute he would laugh and yell "Gotcha," but he just looked off into the distant storm.

"Reefer . . . you talkin' about some Sunday School story?"

Reefer was silent for the longest time, but then he responded in a soft voice, "Yeah, I'm talking about some Sunday School story. Except I'm talking about what really happened, and how I came to be here now."

Eventually, he looked back at me with something like regret in his eyes as if he didn't want to tell me what he was about to. His eyes studied me trying to determine whether I was ready or not or even trustworthy enough to share his secret. Reefer fixed his eyes on mine as he began.

"Do you remember those Sunday School stories about a war in heaven between God and that trickster, Lucifer? That's the war I'm talking about. That war was for control. It was driven by selfishness. It was driven by believing we can make better decisions for ourselves than the One who created us. We all had free will. When the created beings chose sides, I didn't. I used my will to just walk away—to surf, and I been surfing ever since."

Reefer let what he had just revealed sink in before he continued. "We're not in this existence alone. No matter what you believe or don't believe. It all didn't just happen. There are things that went on before all this was made. There was a plan. A plan to create a Paradise for the created ones. But that Trickster, he messed it all up by choosing himself over the Creator. It all went bad then. A choice had to be made. Which side you on? I didn't choose any side. I just left, and there is no goin' back."

He probably could tell by the look on my face that I was processing the ridiculousness of what he had just said and yet, I was curious. There certainly was a mystery to all that happened around Reefer, but an angel or created being or whatever he thinks he is was just too weird!

"Ok, if you are what you say you are, then prove it by doin' some magic, conjure up some spell or somethin'."

Sighing deeply, Reefer said quietly, "I don't do magic. All those things . . . well, they ain't magic as you think. They all happened because of what I am. I made them happen because I'm . . . not a created human. I'm created, I just ain't human. I was created as a part of the heavens, and I can do some things that you humans can't do."

"Reefer, you expect me to believe that you're some sort of guardian angel sent to look after me, like Clarence in that movie?"

"I wasn't sent to look after you! I'm here because I chose to leave, to surf! Aren't you listening? My eternity is here. You're just a part of the history that passes me by, like everyone else, like every day. I hear things, I choose to help sometimes. That's it! *You* get to choose. Me, I made my choice already. But sometimes surfing's not enough anymore. I'm stuck forever since I made that choice. By not picking a side, I've damned myself," Reefer said looking up to the heavens. Then looking back at me, he continued, "It was fantastic at first, all the waves, but after thousands of years . . . well, something's missing.

"The waves . . . well, the waves just aren't big enough anymore."

4

Snorkelin' Through American History

You never know just how beautiful the world is until you're looking up at it from fifteen feet below on the ocean floor. The crystal-clear blue of the water mingling with the cloudless heavens is a sight that few ever take the time to savor. Occasionally a school of pinkish-red and yellow-striped lane snapper or even a couple of queen angelfish swim into sight between you and the surface, interrupting the blue water with their vibrant color of orange and blue stripes. The gentle movement of the current as it massages you along the sand floor in waters that are a mild 80 degrees is so intoxicating that you almost forget that you can't hold your breath forever. Most folks don't have the nerve to lay on an ocean floor fifteen feet down. Most folks fear things that can pinch you, sting you, or eat you at fifteen feet below. But not Michael John or his snorkeling buddy, Dwight. This is their other drug.

Michael John and Dwight have been friends since elementary school. They only lived about five miles apart if you were to cut straight through the pine woods and palmetto thickets. However, depending on the federal government's decision to re-draw district boundaries each year for intergration, there were years from time to time the boys couldn't hang out daily. They initially met in Mrs. Greer's first-grade class and by Miss Franklin's second grade class, they were best friends. Busing kept them apart during the rest of their elementary years. In junior high they were briefly reunited, but it didn't last thanks to the government experiment. Fortunately, by the time they got to high school, things had settled down, and the government was more interested in a war overseas than the war at home.

This story really begins two summers before Michael John's senior year of high school. While on staff at the Boy Scout camp Tanah Keeta, he was given the keys to the handicraft barn and access to all its contents. The camp was supplied by WWII surplus which included everything from K-rations to Willys Jeeps. Rummaging through the leftovers in the upstairs loft, Michael John came across an unopened crate of 48-star flags still in their original packaging. The crate was empty at the end of summer.

Now the summer before his senior year of high school found Michael John already a veteran of the counter-culture and a promising member of the draft card burning army. Many in this community were gifted a 48-star flag for protest purposes. It was not popular among the folks who were loyal to The Man to use the American flag for any other purpose than to display their patriotism. Wearing it as a patch anywhere but on your sleeve or over your breast pocket was considered offensive by his parents' generation. Placing the flag patch on the butt pocket of your Levis' and sitting on it could get you thrown out of many establishments. Wearing clothing that was manufactured to look like the American flag was considered an open declaration of membership in a Marxist leaning society. And to make an article of clothing *from* an American flag was . . . well . . . downright anarchy. Even if that flag was an outdated 48-star flag.

Michael John's "hippie" attire was a mixture of frequent trips to the local Goodwill store and his artistic vision when it came to sewing. He had learned to sew from his older sister while watching her put together her 4-H shifts for the state fair competition.

"I'm not going to sew those stupid patches on a brand-new pair of bell-bottoms," she declared.

"Fine! Just show me how to thread that damn machine, and I'll sew them myself."

Taking the red and white stripes from his flag stash, he made a long-sleeve collarless shirt that slipped on without any buttons. He then took the blue with the white stars and sewed pockets onto his jeans and then inserted a triangular patch of blue and white into each leg below the knee to complete the uniform. Before heading out for the first day of his senior year, called for a current high tide schedule and weather report. This would become his habit each morning.

Dwight picked him up in his '62 Ford Falcon. "Cool shirt," he said as he turned up the 8-track. The speakers blasted out the protest lyrics to a Buffalo Springfield song. They both began to sing along at the top of their lungs as the morning mellow settled in. Michael John relaxed into the seatback as he admired his handiwork on his American flag shirt. Both he and the song continued their vocal protest.

The high school parking lot was a mass of confusion as cars jockeyed for position. Muscle cars upfront, so their owners could flex their machismo. The expensive cars reluctantly took the second position, but the girls used this to their advantage as their perfume lingered longer between cars. And last, the stoners and surfers—a mishmash of whatever moved you from one point to another and looked cool doing it. This is where Dwight parked as he and Michael John hopped out and ran into the building while the tardy bell clanged.

"Michael John, the man. Who ya got for American History? Stan and I got Smith," Kenny asked as he leaned against the hallway lockers. He leaned because standing was rather difficult due to the dizzying effects of some Columbian weed he had smoked in the parking lot in Steve's powder blue 2-door Galaxy. Steve's car didn't need any sun tint on the windows since the inside never seemed to be clear of smoke. "One thing's for sure," he would often declare, "since that scientific report we'll never catch glaucoma. We done had the vaccine."

Looking at his class schedule, Michael John mumbled, "Hmmm, looks like I got Colletta. Americanism versus Communism at 1:30. What do you know about Colletta?"

"What I know," Kenny snorted a laugh over his shoulder as he stumbled down the hall, "is that you better ditch that shirt before you go to class."

"UNTIL YOU TAKE THAT SHIRT OFF YOU GET THE HELL OUT OF MY CLASSROOM!" Mr. Colletta demanded standing in the doorway and waving his index finger out into the hallway. His tone and volume frightened most of the class, and two nerdy students began to remove their double pocket plaid shirts without realizing that Colletta was not yelling at them.

Intimidated by the confrontation, Michael John turned and left without any further protest. High tide was at 2:37 today.

While driving to Boyton Beach, Dwight looked at Michael John and declared, "So, he just threw you out of class. He didn't even let you come in to take roll?"

"No, wouldn't even let me in the door. What's Colletta's deal, man?"

"Don't cha know? He was some sort of former Marine sergeant I hear. I mean, think about it—the flat-top haircut, the spit-shined shoes, and the tattoo on his left forearm. Yeah, I heard he was some kind of war hero. My ol' man told me he got all shot up in D-Day or something while trying to save a bunch of his buddies. Yeah, the guy's a real honest-to-God hero, I hear."

"Well, no war pig is gonna tell me what I can and can't do. This is America, and I got a right to dress any way I want to dress. It's in the

Constitution . . . I think."

Dwight furrowed his brows and glanced at Michael John wondering if it was time Michael John cut back on the weed. He asked, "Say, man, I know you ain't never been a fan of the war and stuff, but what's got you so uptight about Colletta? He's just a dude that did his duty like your ol' man and mine."

Slouching down in the car seat and staring out the window, Michael John pondered before answering. "You know when Rick came back from that Seal boot camp, and we ran the four-forty on the track, and I ran it once, but Rick just kept runnin' and runnin'. He never seemed to tire, and when he did stop, I told him he was just like a robot. A robot, man! He told me that the Military Man turned him into some kinda machine and I could see in his eyes they stole his spirit. Ain't nobody gonna steal my spirit, man. Nobody, you dig!" Michael John declared raising up in his seat and turning to Dwight as he continued.

"When I look at Colletta through his big, black glasses and those bloodshot eyes, I see he's got the same look. He ain't got no spirit. It's like he ain't even there. Like he's stoned without the stone or somethin'. I don't want that gettin' on me."

Dwight nodded, looking straight ahead and said, "I wonder if there's something else that stole Colletta's spirit. I'm trying to remember something my dad said about him, but at the moment I can't recall what it was."

Slouching back down into the seat again, Michael John added, "Man, let's not talk about that right now. I just want to soak up some sun and sink to the bottom lookin' up. Hey, did you bring your gun? I feel like teasin' some 'Cuda?"

Six weeks into the fall term, Dwight got caught by the dean for skipping class. Michael John turned himself in to share the detention with him. The dean was surprised and admitted, "I wasn't even looking for you because your name was never turned in as truant."

It seemed when he walked away from Colletta's class that first day, Colletta assumed he had taken another teacher and simply wrote him off his class roster.

Coming out of detention, Michael John was headed to the parking lot to meet up with Dwight for the 3:17 high-tide when he heard a commanding voice demanding he turn around. Standing outside the building with his back and left foot leaning against the wall and smoking a Lucky Strike cigarette was Colletta. He coughed a little each time he took a puff, but his habit was too strong to quit. As Michael John came close to him, he dropped the cigarette and stood away from the wall rubbing the butt with his left foot. He looked up at Michael John through his Buddy Holly glasses and bloodshot eyes, and that's when a decision was made. He did not give Michael John an option to accept or reject, he simply demanded he come to his office the next day after classes.

Arriving at Colletta's office early—he wasn't going to be late and add to his punishment—Michael John looked around at all the awards hanging on the office walls. It seems he was not only a war hero. There were two awards for Teacher of the Year and awards from the Rotary Club and the Optimist Club. Michael John had no idea the man had accomplished so much. Leaning in and squinting his eyes, he studied a black and white photograph of soldiers and saw a very young Colletta smiling with his arm around another soldier.

A stern voice from behind made Michael John jump as it said, "That was my unit. Great bunch of men. We took that just before we were deployed to Europe," and then with sadness in his voice, Colletta said, "not one of them still alive now. Most of them died over there."

Michael John realized he was seeing a side of the man that he had yet to know. Colletta was the only one left. When he was gone, the photo would all be of ghosts.

"Now here's the deal. You will meet with me every afternoon after sixth period, and we will go over everything that you missed these last six weeks. You will retake every quiz and every test that you missed from that time and pass them with at least a B. If you don't, you will be facing summer school and will not be allowed to graduate with your friends. And one more thing," he said sternly as he leaned close to Michael John poking him several times hard in the chest with his index finger, "Do not, I repeat, do not wear that flag shirt or I will end the deal immediately. You got that?"

"I got it, man, I got it!" Michael John replied as he turned his face away from Colletta's smoke-soured breath. "Say what's your deal with my shirt anyways? You got something against the American flag?"

"Yeah, I got something against using the flag disrespectfully, and cutting it up to make a shirt is pretty damn disrespectful." Standing up and turning toward the picture on his wall, he asked, "Didn't your dad fight in the war?"

"He was in the war, yeah, but he told me that if my time came to get drafted, he would buy me a bus ticket to Canada. He says I ain't got no business goin' to 'Nam. Man, I don't wanna shoot nobody. I ain't mad at them anyways. They got just as much right to live their lives as they want as I do. Makes me no difference. You dig?"

Colletta's blood pressure was rising with each word that Michael John spoke. "How did you kids miss your lessons on patriotism and love for this country. I bet it's because you have it too easy today and your minds are corrupted with all that dope and loud music—if you can call that noise music."

Looking at this skinny, long-haired kid in his cutoffs and sandals, Colletta said with some reluctance, "I have almost half a mind to pull the offer, but then—oh, what the hell. If it ain't you, then it'll be someone else."

It was the Saturday morning of graduation. Colletta had promised to let Michael John know if he was graduating with his classmates by Friday afternoon. He had not called, so Micheal John looked his number up in the phone book and called him.

"Mr. Colletta, this is Michael John. Have you heard anything? Do I get to walk or not?"

There was a bit of silence, and then Colletta replied almost apologetically, "I argued with Dean Jenkins all night last night, and he has not given me a clear answer. I reminded him of the agreement and that you fulfilled your part and passed every quiz and test with at least a B. In fact, I emphasized that the majority of the grades were A's, but Jenkins still refuses to make a decision. All I can tell you is that you should report to graduation in your gown and if they pull you out of the line, well, it's out of my hands, and you'll have to go to summer school."

Michael John felt like he needed to do something to show appreciation for all the history teacher had given and then decided to give him directions to the graduation party out at the shell pits.

"I didn't think you would really come," Michael John said to Colletta while facing him with another 48-star flag draped over his and Mary's shoulders. He offered Colletta the joint he was smoking, but a tired Colletta brushed it off with a wave of his hand and took a swig from the flask he pulled out of his back pocket. He said nothing about the flag.

Colletta turned to address another student who freaked out when he saw the teacher and, confused, quickly hid his beer behind his back.

"You planning on going to college in the fall?" Colletta asked.

The student stuttered unintelligibly and looked around to others for help, but everyone else was just as freaked out.

Colletta smiled at the student as he tipped his flask and took a long swallow. The student dropped his beer.

Tapping Colletta on the shoulder, Michael John asked as he turned to face him again, "Hey, Mr. C, I just gotta know one thing—why me? I know we didn't get along on some things, but . . . why me?"

Colletta looked up with his bloodshot eyes, and with a weak smile, he said after a long hesitation, "Why the hell not."

Tipping his flask toward Michael John, he took one more swig as he turned and walked slowly, his shoulders slumped, into the darkness like a ghost. And only then did Michael John realize he had never really said thank you.

5

Mary, Mother of...

She told him not to empty the kerosene from the stove while he'd been drinkin'. He told her times was hard, and he'd be damned if he was "gonna send the stove back full of kerosene." She told him to take it outside if he had to. He told her he knew what the hell he was doin'. He told her he'd smoked around kerosene 'afore and by hell, he'd never had a problem. "Quit 'chur worrin', Mary," he told her as the ash fell from his lips.

"GET OUT!" he yelled at his children as the flames began to lick up the spilled kerosene. Everywhere he ran in the house yelling for his children his body set more fires.
  "EVERYONE OUT! RUN YOUNGINS! RUN LIKE HELL!"

"Oscar, come out of there! The youngins is all out! OSCAR!"
  "Quickly youngins, roll him in the sugar sand. Put the fire out! Oscar! Oscar don't cha leave me. Oscar, you cain't leave me with all these babies. Oscar! OSCARRR!!!"
  Uncle John was heading toward the flames when he caught three-year-old Nody running down the old shellrock road that Oscar laid

through the swamp. The child was laughing, not understanding the hardship that was chasing him. The child was laughing as he said, "Run like held. Pappy, he says, run like held."

Meanwhile, the other children threw sand in their daddy's face while the world around them grew dark in the glowing embers. And Mary wept.

Hail Mary, full of grace.

Hospitals sometimes just delay death, so here she stood three days later holding Roberta, the newborn, with her other four children looking down into that hole—the new mistress who would forever keep her Oscar from her. The pine box had been closed due to the fire's appetite. Her last image of her Oscar was of oozing bandages and that smell. Oh, that smell. Oscar had broken his promise to never leave. She wouldn't be able to care for all five.

Which one? Which one of her babies would she give up? Jim's the oldest, but he's sickly. Nody still needs his momma. Momma still needed Deannie. Robertas still nursin'. Jr.? Jr., he's the one who needs a daddy the most. He wouldn't like it. He thinks he's the man of the family now, but she can't feed them all. Grandpa can get him to manhood.

"Momma! Don't you love me? Why don't you send Nody or Deannie? They don't know how to do nuthin'. I can build the house again. I can protect you. I can hunt. Momma! Why don't you love me! MOMMMMAA!"

She held the baby tighter as she listened to the screams of her boy driving off with Grandpa. She knew in her heart it was the only thing she could possibly do to make sure Jr. would have a chance in all this hardship.

This was goin' be harder than puttin' the house back together. This was goin' be harder than feedin' her brood. This was goin' be harder than losin'

Oscar. He will hate me forever. He'll never forgive me.

"Oh, Oscar, why did you have to quit us."

I can build the house again. I can protect you. I can hunt. Momma! Why don't you love me! MOMMMAA!"

He will hate me forever. He'll never forgive me.

Hail Mary, full of grace.

Taking stock of the damage, Mary realized that all the windows and doors would have to be replaced. Temporarily she would use tin and burlap bags since money was hard to come by and what did come would have to go to the hospital and other necessities. The furnishings would all have to come from whatever she could beg, scrounge, or make-shift. The inside walls could be recovered with paint and paper to hide the fire's anger. Here and there his footprints could still be seen melted into patches of the linoleum floor. The outside stucco held up against the fire's rape, but the home was forever weakened due to its brutality. Fortunately, the shotgun was spared. It would protect them from the varmints that would surely intrude, both animal and human. It also would provide for the table. Gathering the children to her in what remained of the living room that first night, Mary wrapped them in borrowed blankets and cradled the baby in one arm and the shotgun in the other. The sun had now set outside, but the darkness inside the house was not just from the lack of light.

Oh, Oscar, why did you have to quit us.

I can build the house again. I can protect you. I can hunt. Momma! Why don't you love me! MOMMMAA!"

He will hate me forever. He'll never forgive me.

Hail Mary, full of grace.

"Mary. Let me in, Mary," the ol' drunk yelled as he banged on the tin windows. "Come on Mary I know'd you's in there. Come on out and dance in the moonlight. I know'd you's ain't danced since poor 'ol Oscar got eat up by that there fire. Come on Mary, it'll do you some good."

"Now Lester, you go on and get away from this house. I got my youngins in here, and they's all asleep. Go on now and get or so help me I'll pepper your hide with buckshot through this here tin. I'm a warnin' you, Lester!"

"Maarrry."

BOOMMM!!!

It had to be them Westgate boys. Mary knew they were no count. She loaded up her brood in the ol' Hudson and drove to the west county line. Cradling the shotgun in one arm and Roberta in the other, Mary hollered into the house, "Bobby C, them worthless no count boys of yours' done stole gas from me and I aim to get it back! Now march one of them out here, or I start shootin' up the place."

"Boys! Did you steal from Miss Mary? Get the hell on out there and put it back and give her some extra. What? I don't no more care if'n she does pepper your worthless hides. Do it!"

Oh, Oscar why did you . . . .

I can build the house again. I can protect you. I can hunt. Momma! Why don't you love me!"

He will hate me forever. He'll never forgive me.

Hail Mary, full of grace.

"Mary, where'd you get such a mess of birds? Looks like Christmas done come early," Aunt Mabel asked with suspicion.

"Oh, I just wait till they all line up on the phone wire, that way I only need one shot. Shells is hard to come by nowadays."

Looking at the feathers scattered in the back grass, "Mary, you got any notion what them birds was?"

"The eatin' kind. Why?"

"That there is a mess of Florida state birds. There's a fine for shootin' 'em. 'Round a thousand dollars a bird."

After offering thanks for the bountiful meal before them, Mary said, "Eat up youngins. There's six thousand dollars worth of meat on the table. Don't leave nuthin' but bones."

I can build the house again. I can protect you. I can hunt. Momma! Why don't you . . . !"

He will hate me forever. He'll never forgive me.

Hail Mary, full of grace.

He was more than fifteen now. A fine, strong young man. Grandpa had done his work, but now he's gone to the earth to join Grandma. Mary stood in the doorway with a new baby in one arm and watched as Jr. came up the old shellrock road.

"This here's your baby brother, Paul. Haskel, he's a good man. He strengthened the house where it was weak. My how you have growed, son. Will you stay for a while?"

"There's a war on Mama. I'll stay till next summer. I can sleep on the back porch."

He could have built the house again. He could have protected us. He could have hunted. Will he hate me forever? Will he ever forgive me?

Hail Mary.

6

Love You, Crazy

Ever wonder what it's like being insane? I'm not talking about induced psychosis. You know, that kind of crazy that Leary and Alpert did at Harvard in the 60s with LSD. No, I'm talking about honest-to-goodness crazy in the brain because there's some chemical imbalance, or some synapse is not firing correctly. The kind of crazy that has you screaming in the corner of a room full of people and you can't stop it. The kind of crazy that Teri went through that night so long ago in Daniel's apartment. The kind of crazy that got her committed to the Florida State Hospital in Chattahoochee, Florida. That's the kind of crazy I'm talking about. But I'm getting ahead of myself.

Stan's my best friend. Always has been. Always will be. He was my protector. My bodyguard. When I was in elementary school, I was constantly the kid every bully and everyone that wanted to bully picked on. That is, until I met Stan. Stan immediately liked me, and so the word spread that to mess with me meant you messed with Stan. Stan could back it up too. If he needed help, which rarely he did, he had four brothers who would back him up. Stan was the keeper of the secrets that only best friends share. He knew that *I didn't* when I told everyone I did.

Best friends are like that. He was the closest thing to a blood brother I ever had. And Stan felt the same about me. Hell, even in his family I was considered the sixth brother and the seventh child—there was a sister. Stan's mom was my *other mother*. I called her Mom. She covered for me with my own mother when I was not where I was supposed to be. She even changed my name.

She said, "If you had been my son by birth, I'd have named you Michael John."

So I am Michael John or MJ to this day.

Like I said, Stan and I were tight. We even shared the same girlfriends. When one of us for whatever reason ended a relationship, the other—with a blessing—would sometimes step in and continue the relationship. That's what happened when Stan ended his relationship with Teri. I stepped in, but again I get ahead of myself.

Teri had a past in crazy. A past that neither Stan nor I knew about. People Teri grew up around knew her past crazy, but no one ever clued us in. Stan met Teri at Daniel's apartment. She was from Daniel's hometown in central Florida. Looking back on it now, Daniel should have told us about her, but I guess, maybe, he thought she was fine as long as she was on her meds. Trouble came when Teri decided on her own to quit following the doctor's orders and went off her meds. It was the early 70s, and there were plenty of *drugs* out there for almost any condition. At least that's what we all thought. Teri thought she could manage her descent into crazy with a little pot and maybe some downers. Teri was wrong.

One night at Daniel's apartment we had gathered to listen to the new *Kiss* album. Daniel was convinced this was the best album he had ever heard. I liked the idea of makeup, but the music didn't interest me. Stan and Teri were over in the corner talking, and Teri looked visibly upset. She cowered below Stan and then crumbled to the floor with a screeching wail that I first thought was coming from the album. Daniel turned immediately and recognized Teri's crazy scream since he had heard it before many times.

"Stan, what the hell did you do to the woman?" I shouted, laughing over the music. I didn't realize yet that the scream had originated in her head and had to find a way out. Stan just stared at me with a look of horror.

Daniel moved quickly and tried to get Teri to focus on him, believing that the recognition would be helpful in settling her down.

"Teri, look at me. It's Daniel, Teri. Remember? We went to high school together. Remember?"

It wasn't working. Her screaming intensified. Stan looked like he was ready to run; I thought about running with him.

Someone, I don't know who—called someone; I don't know who—and after about 30 to 40 minutes of screaming Teri's sister came in and with the help of Daniel got Teri out and into a car. As they drove away, I could still hear the screaming.

It was several days later that Stan learned Teri had been committed to the Florida State Hospital. He asked if I wanted to go along with him to visit her. During the drive, Stan was unusually quiet, and it was not because of the Jamaican weed we had just smoked.

I finally asked, "You bummed 'cause of Teri?"

Looking slowly at me as if he was unaware anyone was in the seat next to him—probably the result of the Jamaican—he finally spoke.

"Yeah."

We drove for miles before I asked, "Is she gonna be ok?"

"Don't know." We drove the rest of the way in silence. It was a silence that did not prepare us for what we were about to see.

When we arrived at the institution, I was struck by how old and creepy the building felt. I later learned it was built in the 1870s and was Florida's first mental institution. Originally it was used as an arsenal for the Seminole Indian Wars. It was later it became an institution for the mentally insane. I read somewhere that it housed some notable characters. One was Victor Licata, an ax murderer, who was convicted, so the police said, because he was a pot addict. The courts used this case to suggest that the use of pot could be linked to criminal intent. Of course, this is bullshit. Me and Stan have been smoking for years, and I can't think of one time either of us took an ax to anyone. The worse we done is pilfered a bag of Munchos from the local 7-11.

After parking, we found the front door, and I noticed Stan hesitated with his hand on the door handle for what seemed like a long time. I put my hand on his and helped him turn it. He turned to me with a look that said he was at a loss and didn't know what he would do or say. When we stepped inside, we were immediately disoriented due to the dark lighting. A single bulb hung suspended from a long wire coming from the ceiling. Only one of the fluorescent fixtures was working, and it flickered off and on but provided no constant light. There was a little light coming in from a couple of small windows near the front door. I noticed they were nailed shut. There were a few pieces of worn furniture for visiting in the wide foyer. It was walled on three sides with the open-end spilling into a large high-ceilinged expanse that had only a single structure in the middle. It was a glass-walled booth in an octagon shape that had only one door and a small window with heavy mesh wire acting as a barrier from those outside the booth. This appeared to be where visitors checked in. There was no sign. The enclosure was inhabited by several nurses in white starch uniforms looking unhappy about the two long-hairs who just walked into their quiet sanctuary. Stan cautiously approached the window, and a smile-less nurse looked up at him waiting for him to explain why he was standing there. No greeting. No welcome to the Florida State Hospital for the mentally crazy. Not even a 'what the hell do you two hippies want'?

Stan leaned down to the wire mesh and told the nurse we were here to see Teri. The nurse grumbled something as she checked her clipboard and then, looking at Stan and around him at me, told us to have a seat in the foyer. They would send for her.

We waited on the one couch in the foyer for what seemed like an unusually long and unnecessary period of time. It was as if the nurses delayed bringing Teri to us, perhaps in hopes that we would get discouraged and leave. Finally, Teri appeared from somewhere down a long hall accompanied by a nurse whose sneakered shoes squeaked as she followed Teri. Once the nurse reached the glass booth, she turned and entered and then wrote on a clipboard as she whispered something to the other nurses. They all looked up at once toward us. Teri did not smile as she came tentatively toward us and looked around as if she were searching for the right place to sit. Finally, she sat down between us without any embrace or even a pleasant greeting of "good to see you." She just sat there rubbing her hands as she stared silently at the floor.

Fumbling in the silence, Stan finally asked, "How they treatin' you here?"

Teri slowly eyed Stan with a look that expressed her surprise he would ask such a question. Didn't he understand what it was like to be incarcerated in such a dreary place as this?

"How are they treating me? Are you crazy?" she declared.

Without thinking and trying to break the awkwardness of the moment, I offered, "No, you are. That's why you're here."

Teri peered at me with fear in her eyes, and I thought for a moment that she was going to repeat the screaming episode that got her here. But she just lowered her head and stared at the floor again while muttering weakly that she was sorry. Sorry for what I wasn't sure. Sorry for being crazy? I couldn't blame her. It wasn't her fault. At least, that's what I kept telling myself. I mean if I had to stay locked up here, I know I would never be uncrazy. This place was not helping her. Stan knew it too.

After some more awkward silence, I heard what sounded like glass breaking coming from down the hall from which Teri had just come. Her head shot up with terror in her eyes as several nurses rushed from their guard enclosure, all carrying twisted sheets and running down the hall.

I asked Teri, "What are they gonna do, tie someone to their bed?"

Teri lowered her head again and whispered, "Yes."

After that the visit was over. There was nothing left to say, so I hugged Teri goodbye.

Stan just turned and walked away without saying anything.

We drove home in silence. Both of us trying to reconcile what we just experienced. I twisted up a number and offered Stan a hit, but he just waved it off. Stan had never waved off a joint—ever!

Mom asked us how Teri was doing. We told her of the sound of broken glass and the nurses with twisted sheets. Mom decided then and there that we needed to spring Teri from her prison. She said what the girl needed was to be around those that loved her. I noticed Stan had turned his head and stared off down the hallway. I suspected Stan was falling out of love with Teri. He didn't know how to live around her at the moment. We were often crazy ourselves, but this was something different. Teri's crazy was not self-induced.

Mom worked her "mom magic" with her special wand, the phone. Mom had a way that Stan and I never understood. When she picked up the phone, things just got done. Somehow, she located and spoke to Teri's parents, who were out of the country at the time. Somehow, she convinced them to grant her temporary custody until they returned. Somehow, she persuaded Teri's doctor that the best thing for Teri's mental health was to allow her to live with us. Mom assured the doctor that Teri's meds would be given properly and that she would have regular visits to his office.

The next morning Stan and I headed back north to Chattahoochee.

For the next couple of weeks, Teri moved slowly and quietly through the house. She often slept with Stan's sister. There were times Stan and I would come home and find her asleep on the couch. We just left her there. More and more, I watched Stan distance himself from Teri. She attempted to generate affection, but he just was unable to respond. I noticed my feelings for her were growing. It wasn't just a sympathy for her condition, I found myself thinking of her before her crazy. I had always liked Teri and was even a little jealous when Stan first started dating her. But I had not heard Stan say she was no longer his girl. I knew it was coming, but I needed him to say it first. I really wanted to be with her. She might be crazy, but Teri was damn cute!

Now let me say something about the management of Teri's mental health with the meds the doctor had her on. Stan and I came home one afternoon and found Stan's brother Brad plastered to the big brown easy chair in the living room. He couldn't move and had a really hard time speaking, but when he did all he could muster was to raise one hand and utter, "Damn, Teri's got some powerful downers." After that we got Mom to call her doctor, and after working her mom magic again, she got Teri's meds reduced.

Teri slowly began to lose her crazy.

One evening I had crashed early in the bunk below Stan's. Now the rule was for the boys: whoever got home first got a bed. There were not enough for all of us with me as part of the family. Many a time someone of blood slept on the floor because I was in their bed. This particular night Teri came in quietly to the room. I suspected she was looking for Stan, but he hadn't made it home yet from work. When she realized it was me, she slid in next to me under the sheets.

After a long silence, she whispered, "Do me."

Dope has a funny way of creating realities that are mostly wanna be realities. You know the kind that you tell stories about years later to make your past sound like it was something to behold. It impresses those who didn't even though they say they did. I stared at her in the darkness looking for something in her face that convinced me she had just given me what every guy wishes for—permission without strings. Surely, I misunderstood. After all, I was pretty stoned when I crashed, but then she whispered again, "Do me, please."

Now that time I heard clearly what she said. I wondered if it was her meds talking or maybe that crazy part of her had gotten out again. If it was the crazy part, I wondered if she would be hacking me up after we did it? I actually thought for a moment if it would be worth it to have sex and then have my head split open by an ax. Man, I thought—what a rush that would be! Teri's crazy had nothing on my crazy.

Just as I decided to give in to my base nature, the door opened up again. Standing there with the hall light shining behind like a halo all around was Jesus! At least that's who I thought was standing there. Later when my buzz wore off, I realized it was Stan's brother Rutt with his long brown hair and beard. But at the moment I was convinced the Son of God had come to stop me from *doin'* Teri. I didn't have Stan's blessing, so I turned from Teri and pretended to go to sleep. She slowly got out of bed and walked past Jesus. He crawled into Stan's bed.

The next morning, I rushed out to work, avoiding Teri out of embarrassment for the both of us. I wasn't sure if it was an embarrassment on my part for not doin' her or embarrassment on her part for asking and not getting what she wanted. I met up with Stan later that afternoon at the beach to body-surf. I was determined to know where he stood with Teri. I needed his blessing.

"Man, you and Teri still gettin' it on or what?"

Stan looked up at the blue sky from the blue water and then at me. "I don't know how to handle crazy. I guess it's over."

That was it! He was giving me the go-ahead. And I was going to take it. Next time she said, "do me," I would.

But the next time never came.

One morning several days later, Teri and I were alone in the house. She was sitting on the couch as I came out of the shower. I sat down with her in my towel, hoping she might wanna do it.

"How you doin' babe? You wanna head to the beach or somethin'?"

Teri looked straight ahead and breathed a deep sigh. Then she began to speak quietly as she lowered her head, and tears began to form in her eyes.

"Being crazy sucks."

"Yeah, I know whatcha mean," I said as I glanced at her with an attempt at understanding.

Raising her eyes, she asked, "Do you? Do you really understand what crazy is, that you ain't got no control? You ain't never been insane. Not like this where you can't shut it off? You don't know shit."

"Yeah, I know my crazy don't compare to yours, but I got demons too. My dope-crazy is just a way to silence them."

She looked into my eyes for some recognition of my experience with hers and then as if a light went on, she smiled slightly and nodded in agreement that we all got a little crazy. Some just more than others.

"Do you think we'll ever be sane," she asked as she gently laid her head on my shoulder.

"I don't know. I don't know how long crazy lasts."

7

Snake Handlers on the Pike

T he Florida Turnpike, also known as the Sunshine Parkway—or just the Pike to locals—runs up the center of the state from Florida City in the south to Wildwood in the north where one can pick up I-75 heading into Georgia. For a hitchhiker, the Pike is preferable to the coastal highways since once you get a ride, it usually does not stop until you get to the end. All you gotta do is stand outside and away from the tollbooth (pedestrians are not allowed on a turnpike) and just raise your thumb. The Pike will do the rest.

But nowadays a hitchhiker has to be cautious about who offers a ride. It seems that more and more, the roads are filling up with psychopaths like the Santa Rosa killer or perverts who might try to practice some of their weird fantasies on an unsuspecting rider. It's difficult to exit a vehicle at 70 miles an hour down the asphalt when a rider senses trouble. Now the best ride by far comes from a long hair in a VW. They still believe in love and peace and dope. Another good ride is a vehicle full of adults, no children—they ask too many questions. So, when the hitchhiker saw a car with four men and Tennessee plates, he figured it would be a good ride all the way to the end of the Pike.

Rolling down the front passenger's window, a dark-tanned, skinny-

55

faced man with oily hair, brown-stained teeth, and liquor breath asked, "Need a ride there, fella'? We's headed back ta home. Welcome ta join us."

"Yeah, thanks. I appreciate it," the hitcher replied as he opened the back passenger door of the rusted '58 Buick station wagon. A tall, sweaty, bulky man in faded Big Smith overalls, no shirt, and hair cut close to the scalp on the sides looked rather annoyed as he slowly lifted himself out from the back seat to let the new rider slide into the middle. The car actually raised up as he got out. Sliding in and straddling the transmission hump while holding his duffle bag in his lap, the hitcher kicked a burlap sack tied with a piece of string on the floor. He swore he saw the bag move.

"Throw your stuff in the back there," Overalls muttered without looking at the hitcher and pointing with his thumb over his shoulder. He then took a long swallow of what looked like water in a quart Mason jar. Thinking this ride could be trouble, the hitcher quickly considered jumping out, but to do so, he would have to climb over Overalls' sweaty, no-shirt, fat body that hid the door handle somewhere in his massive frame. Anyway, the opportunity was gone when the driver, who was wearing an old, stained, black Fedora, pulled quickly back onto the highway causing the oncoming traffic to slam on their brakes and switch lanes dangerously while blowing their horns. The driver took no time getting the station wagon up to the posted speed limit and then some.

Turning in the front seat and offering a hand with dirty fingernails and numerous double puncture scars, the skinny, oily-haired man said drunkenly, "Name's Jereemiuh, where's it you's a-headin'?"

Without thinking, the hitcher said, "Gainesville." Now if he hadn't been so nervous, he should have said he was going only to the next exit, but it was too late. Oh well, might as well try and relax and enjoy the ride, he thought, besides they might offer him a sip from that jar the nervous young boy next to the other backseat window was now tipping up and guzzling. Somehow, Overalls passed the jar without giving the hitcher a chance at it. The boy didn't look like he was more than fifteen or sixteen years old, at best. His face was full of pimples with a few patches of hair along his jawline that did not connect, mostly sprouting from his chin. There also was a noticeable fresh swollen cut on his lip. He smelled of hours-old-sweat; in fact, it was impossible not to notice that they all smelled of south Florida sweat, and the hitcher was fairly certain there wasn't a can of Right Guard anywhere in the car. When the split-lipped boy raised the jar again, the Fedora wearing driver looked back from the rearview mirror and yelled at him, "Geez, Micah you gonna drink the whole damn jar afore we gets to the state line. Pass that there 'shine up here. NOW, BOY!"

"Now, Brother Aaron, where's yore manners. We got's company. Don't cha think it would be Christian charity to offer our new rider here a sample?" Jeremiah said as he looked back at the cautious hitcher, giving him a wink with one of his bloodshot eyes.

Micah was torn between doing what Aaron demanded and what Jeremiah suggested. He was visibly worried that he wouldn't make the right choice and either choice would result in consequences from the demanding driver. Touching his lip Micah hesitantly started to hand the jar to the front seat, but then changed his mind and handed it to the hitcher. Then he slumped down in the seat quickly and pushed his head back into the vinyl to avoid any retaliation from the front.

"Let me do the introductions," Jeremiah offered. "This fat feller here on your right is Zack, that's short for Zachariah, and next to you on the other side that there is Micah. And this mean one here drivin' is Aaron. So, what'd you go by?"

"I'm MJ. It's . . . it's short for Michael John."

"Well, ain't that nice; we's all got names from the Good Book." Pointing around to each rider, Jeremiah declared, "We here are all members of the Reverend Hensley's church. You ever hear'd of Brother

George Went Hensley?"

MJ shook his head slowly from side to side.

Jeremiah leaned over the front seat and with a forced grin continued, "We's Pentecostal Holiness. Been to a camp meetin' down ta Bartow. Headin' back to Chattanooga. Now I gotta ask, ya see it's my Christian duty, ya got the Holy Ghost in ya?"

With a devious chuckle, the driver whispered in a growl, "There's one way to tell for sure. Have him reach in that there gunny sack full of snakes, and we'll all know for sure."

"Now Brother Aaron, we don't want to go and risk killin' off our guest 'afore we gets the chance to know about his eternal soul, do we? 'Sides this here 'shine we's drinkin' is liable to set the Lord His self into a temper. You know'd He don't take kindly to drinkin'. Don't cha remember what He done at that camp meetin' with that drunk feller what wondered up with that skinny gal. Why He judged him right there in front of us all with that big rattler. One bite right there 'tween the eye and cheek and he went down all a-shakin' and frothin' at the mouth. We like to never got that skinny gal to quit all her screamin'. Why if'n Zach here hadn't smacked her on the jaw and shut her up, then we'd still be in Bartow 'stead of headin' back ta home. No sir, what was it the preacher said, he said we's to be more gracious and more open to the unwashed and stop throwin' serpents at new folks to see if'n they's part of the brethren."

"I like the throwin' and smackin'. Gets straight to the knowin' for sure," Zachariah muttered while staring out the window into the growing darkness.

"Not you too Brother Zach, you know'd that ain't what the preacher said was gonna work anymore if'n we want to bring in more converts to the family. We got's to use . . . what was it, Brother Aaron, that word the preacher used?"

"Diplomacy," Aaron muttered with an irritated tone.

"Diplomacy. Yeah, that's it. Diplomacy. Yeah, that's what the preacher said. He said if'n we don't stop judgin' new 'nitiates, then the Kingdom ain't-a gonna expand," Jeremiah said, exaggerating with his arms spreading out wide to those in the back seat. "Diplomacy, that's what we's got to do." Dropping his arms and looking puzzled, he turned back to the driver and asked, "Say, Aaron, what's this here word diplomacy mean anyhow?"

Looking from under the brim of his hat, Aaron snarled, "Jeezus, Jeremiah, you as dumb as a sack full of cowshit. Don't you know nuthin'?"

At that same time, Aaron turned in his seat as he yelled, "WHERE THE HELL IS THAT JAR?"

He tried to grab Micah by his shirt, but Micah planted his feet on the floorboard and pushed himself further back into the seat. Unfortunately, he stepped on the bag of snakes and set them to hissing, rattling, and moving all at once. There were fangs poking through the burlap, and wet spots of venom started appearing on the bag as the snakes bit through trying to get revenge for being stepped on. The bag became animated and started to move around the floor causing everyone in the back seat to raise their feet. This was quite a spectacle, especially for Overalls as his massive weight shift crushed MJ pinning him to the seat and blocking his view of where the bag of snakes actually was at the moment. All he could do was scream and kick his legs up in the air, hoping they didn't come in contact with that sack.

"Everyone quiet down back there," Jeremiah pleaded as he raised his feet and leaned away from the backseat, "Brother Aaron, maybe you better pull on over and let's get them snakes where they ain't so jumpy."

"I ain't-a pullin' over until we needs pushin' water." Looking into the rearview mirror, he shouted angrily, "Y'all settle down back there and them there snakes will do the same. Now hand me that jar up here!"

As everyone slowly and cautiously got quiet, the snakes indeed began to do the same. Overalls shifted back to his side of the seat, and MJ was finally able to breathe again. He still didn't trust his feet next to the gunny sack, so he kept them on top of the transmission hump with his arms locked around them so he could pull them up if the bag moved again.

After about an hour of driving in silence, they came to the Wildwood exit and got off the Pike. Aaron said they now needed "pushin' water," so he turned into a Sunoco gas station. Jeremiah suggested everyone get out and stretch their legs. Overalls was slow to exit, and MJ grew anxious as he planned his escape away from these hillbillies and their snakes. He reached over the backseat to grab his duffle while moving in one motion out and around the big man. Jeremiah tipped his head toward Zachariah, and with his narrowed eyes asked MJ if he was planning on leaving their company. Knowing that he better be quick, MJ thanked everyone as he backed away and throwing the duffle over his shoulder, he headed off away from the gas station in a trot looking for another ride up I-75 to Gainesville. The snake handlers did not follow him.

Eventually, he caught a ride with an 18-wheeler that dropped him off at Old Archer Road, the road that would take him to the university. Thanking the driver as he stepped out, MJ immediately noticed how quiet and lonely this part of Old Archer Road was. You could hear the night sounds, a little unnerving after his experience with the snake handlers. MJ shouldered his duffle and began to walk in the direction of town. He noticed there were no streetlights. Walking along in the dark, he was surprised when he happened upon a taxi cab parked on the side of the road with no lights except the glow from the radio. Walking by the driver's window, he could hear Clapton singing "Cocaine." Turning down the music, the long-haired driver leaned out the window and asked, "Say, man, you headed to the university? Want a ride?"

"Nah, I ain't got the bread. I'll just walk."

"Hey, man, no charge. I'm just out here being mellow, diggin' on the crickets. Sometimes the city lights are just too much. I'll give you a ride as long as I don't get no call. Climb on in, dude. Us long-hairs got to stick together."

Throwing his duffle in the back, MJ thanked the cab driver and settled into the seat relaxing for the first time since he got out of the snake handler's station wagon.

Turning up the radio, the driver turned his head toward the rearview mirror and said to the rider in the back seat, "Cocaine must be in town. Every time a shipment shows up, they request this song over and over. You can always tell what major dope is in town by what's playin' on the radio—'The Needle and the Damage Done,' 'Sweet Leaf,' 'Purple Haze.'" Noticing the silence from the backseat, the taxi driver asked, "Say, you ok man? Awful quiet back there."

MJ turned from staring out the window to look at the driver in the rearview mirror and quietly said, "Had a rough ride up the Pike with a car full of drunk snake handlers. They were awful concerned about my soul. Concerned so much that one of them wanted to stick my hand in a bag full of rattlesnakes just to see if I knew their god. Man, it was totally freaky."

"That ain't cool," said the taxi driver. Looking again at the backseat from the rearview mirror, the driver asked with a smile, "Do you believe in God?"

Surprised, MJ replied, "Yeah, I believe there's something out there. Something or somebody had to make all this shit. Just not sure what it is." And then MJ asked, "What do you believe, man?"

Pausing before replying and with a deep sigh, the taxi driver eventually responded, "I think we got off track a long time ago and started inventing stuff to pacify our uncertainty. I think deep inside, we really want something to be in charge of it all, but we don't seem to be able to to agree on how we ought to express our beliefs. I do know one thing, and that is that we can't force it on others because then the path to someone else's reality is never truly our own. We just end up accepting that reality because we are afraid of snakes."

Grinning, he looked in the mirror back at the hitcher.

Staring back out the rear window, MJ sighed, pondering what he just heard. Then turning forward again, he asked, "So how do you think we can know what is true and what is not?"

Again, meeting MJ's eyes with his own in the rearview mirror, the taxi driver smiled and said, "This is truth—love don't hate, man. Love don't hate."

The moment was interrupted by the crackling of the driver's CB radio informing him he had a fare to pick up. Pulling over, the driver let MJ out and wished him peace. And as he drove off, the taxi driver turned up the radio again as the final notes of Clapton's guitar spilled out the open windows and filled the night.

Watching him drive off into the darkness, MJ noticed a glow around the driver's head. Surely, it was the glow from the radio.

8

Please Leave

"Hey, take a walk with me," Sarah's uncle said.

When I looked back over my shoulder at Sarah, she smiled and indicated with a nod that it would be okay to 'take a walk' with her uncle down the old cemetery road in Sweetwater, Tennessee.

Sarah and her family had gathered for an annual cemetery day of cleaning around the gravestones and placing flowers on her grandparents's graves. It seems here in these mountains that they take the honoring of those that have gone on before them seriously. They even take pictures of the dead laid out in their caskets—a fact I learned while thumbing through Sarah's family photo album. When I came to the picture of her granddad with eyes shut and hands folded lying in his casket, I freaked. I threw the album across the room and jumped up hollering who would do such a thing. Sarah narrowed her eyes at me and replied, "We do."

I didn't know that.

Sarah's uncle scared the hell out of me. I silently prayed as we started down the hill that I would return unscathed. I had heard about the many animals that "took" a walk with him, and only he returned. At least he wasn't carrying his rifle.

I probably should tell you at this point that I am from South Florida. I met Sarah one weekend when her other uncle, who I work for, decided to make a quick run-up to Tennessee for a family reunion. He introduced me to Sarah when we played a volleyball game across a barbwire fence used as a net. Sarah had been married to some jerk who I heard had left her for dope. He also left her with a baby. Sarah was a pretty, slim, strawberry-blonde girl who wore her jeans well. I was immediately smitten by her beautiful blue-gray eyes and her independence. She played volleyball with one hand for the volleyball and the other for her baby on her hip. What a woman!

We started a relationship that lasted over the next year or so. I often saw Sarah on the weekend runs to Tennessee, or occasionally she and her baby made the trip down to South Florida. In '75 I took three months off to travel the country in my '71 forest green VW Beetle with driftwood bumpers. Of course, I spent a lot of time with Sarah when I found myself anywhere near her state, which was easy to do since Tennessee was always in the middle of my routes. We became closer, and I began to entertain the idea of settling down in Tennessee. At least, that's what I thought would be a good way to save gas in this long-distance relationship. It's not what her uncle thought though.

As I shuffled down the gravel-top cemetery road, I was overwhelmed once again by the beauty of this state. With its hills and valleys and foggy mornings, I came to love the terrain about as much as I loved Sarah. But her uncle was a hard and angry-looking man with gray hair on the sides of his head and a beer-belly that pushed his trousers down below his waist. The hardness showed in his hands that were scarred and knotted from all the years of working his land, and the anger in his face showed an attitude of indifference. I mean, he had no problem dispatching animals who were no longer useful. That same attitude suggested he wouldn't have a problem getting rid of me, deeming me useless. Seems that attitude is common up here in the Smokies.

I didn't know that.

He was also a man who didn't talk much except to close family members. I would often see him in gatherings lean in close to his brother's ear and whisper some dark conspiracy to him while nodding toward me. Or at least that's what I thought he was doing. Today was no different in that he said nothing to me as we walked. After all, I was not family, and I was certain he was going to make sure that it stayed that way. I figured he be "damned" if he was going to let a long-hair move in with his niece and settle down.

While we walked along in silence, in order to ease my nervousness, I began to relive the events of the last few months. In particular, a couple of months ago when Sarah's younger brother rolled my Beetle. Now here in this rural community, everyone in the family helps when it comes to the operation of the farm. It is not unusual for dads to send sons to town in the family truck for seed or fencing or some other necessary from the local Ace Hardware. Most sons were not old enough to have a license. But in this mountain community, the sheriff is your neighbor and also your Little League coach, so even though they are aware of a boy's age, they look the other way. After all, if a dad had to stop plowing to go fetch some seed, then work would stop.

Send the boy.

I didn't know that.

Sarah's brother had been bugging me to let him drive my VW. He had only seen one once in his life, and that was on a trip to Nashville. He said it was yellow and smoked a lot. So did I—not the car—I smoked a lot of weed, so my judgment was not all that acute that day. I gave in to the idea of an early morning drive through the mountains while the fog was still clinging to the ground. It was like driving in a fantasy land. I thought, what could it hurt? The boy drove his father's truck all the time, so he must know what he's doing.

"Here take a hit of this. Be careful, don't drop it! Shit! Watch the road! I'll find the joint! Shit!"

The Beetle had a mind of its own when no one was driving. It crossed the road and slid on to its side into a gully. No one was hurt, but when I told Sarah's brother not to worry, my insurance would cover any damage, he asked, "Even if the driver ain't got no license?"

"Shit! You ain't got no license! I didn't know that. I seen you drivin' your daddy's truck every day."

"Everyone out here drives as soon as they can reach the pedals. I'm only fourteen. I got two years before I get a license."

"Well, crap! Ok. Let's change seats before the cops get here, and I'll take the —."

"Why don't you tell me just what yur intentions are with my niece?" The voice shook me out of the remembrance and back into the reality that this might be my Dead Man Walking moment. I better be careful with my answer. Thank goodness I hadn't had time to roll that second joint this morning. My mind was fairly clear.

"Well, I like her. I really do. And I like her daughter. We get along well. So, I was thinkin' me and my dog might settle down here and grow me a crop or somethin'.'"

Wrong answer.

I didn't know that.

"Grow a crop! You talkin' 'bout that there Marywanna? Boy, let me tell ya, most folks around here don't take kindly to you outsiders. 'Specially you hippies with yur long hair and loud music and strange ideas 'bout war and stuff."

I started to slow my walk a bit so as to let him get ahead of me. I figured I could outrun this hillbilly if I had a jump on him. He clearly didn't approve of my intentions towards his niece, and I was too afraid to tell him I meant a crop of lettuce and potatoes. Although, the thought had crossed my mind about the richness of the soil and the pot I could grow. But for now, I was just thinking of being near Sarah.

"Listen here, boy. I belong to a certain men's social group, if you know what I mean," he said as he moved toward me and leaned in close to my face with his mountain whiskey breath. "And they don't like the idea of certain folks settlin' here. Oh, we tolerate ol' dark Joe down ta mill, but he and his people go way back 'afore the war—you know the big blue and gray skirmish we had 'while back. Now it seems all you hippies want to settle and live off the land. Ha! Your kind ain't got no understandin' how to make this land feed ya. You'd starve inside a month, and then you all would be runnin' around lookin' for a handout and smokin' that there dope and messin' up yur brains on that shit. No, we don't like yur kind, and we don't intend to let any of y'all settle here. Now, Sarah is my niece, and I like's her a lot and that their baby of hers, too. We ran off that no count husband of hers and we intend to do the same with you. I'll give you a couple of days out of respect for Sarah, but you better put Tennessee in yur rearview mirror by then. You understand me, boy!"

This last bit he emphasized rather loudly, and I wondered if the folks back up at the cemetery could hear. I also wondered if they cared. I knew Sarah would, but her family was tight, and I wasn't sure how much they manipulated her. After all, they ran off her husband! Now it seems that I was being asked to leave by a racist men's social club. I was asked to leave, and they didn't even say please.

"Well, I don't know what to tell you," Sarah said, "but my uncle and his buddies are mighty persuasive. They don't fool around. Not that I want you to, but maybe you should head back south for a while. I can come down later."

Sarah's eyes showed concern, but not so much for what her uncle might do, but for what she hadn't told me yet.

"There might be another reason for you to go. My ex-husband knows about you, and it seems he is lookin' for you."

"Sarah, I ain't afraid of your ex-husband. I can take care of myself. Besides he's never met me. How's he gonna know what I look like?"

"You're not hard to spot in a town so small. You're the only long-hair in Sweetwater. Everyone knows I'm dating a surf bum from South Florida. You drive a VW Beetle with driftwood bumpers and a surf rack and a Florida license plate. And you wear cut-offs with the pockets hangin' out in the front and that cute butt of yours hangin' out the back," she offered with a bit of sarcasm while reaching behind me and squeezing one of those cute butt cheeks.

"Now I like my cute surf bum, but honey, you do stick out in this here mountain town. And besides my ex is known to carry a gun. I think you oughta leave. Please! Please leave."

Well, needless to say, I loaded up the Beetle that afternoon along with my dog and headed out. A few joints into the run south, I started thinking about my leaving without any "Hell, no, I won't go!" I was not that crazy about standing up to some ex-husband with a gun. Sarah's uncle, the man I work for, did that, and the jealous ex shot him in the belly. It took a while for him to get over that. It left him a little gun shy. It left me a whole lot gun shy! I'd like to think I could've stood up to the uncle; however, no telling what the "men's social club" had planned for me if I had stayed.

Sarah and I eventually drifted apart due to the distance. I heard her ex-husband got arrested again, and this time he is doing a stretch in prison. I also heard her uncle was shot and killed in the bed of a woman that was not his wife.

I look back on those days and wonder what different choices would have made of my life. I'd like to think I could have given Sarah the life and the love she deserved. I'd like to think I could have made her happy. I like to think she would have made me happy. But who knows how it would have turned out? She may have had my picture in her family album and would have been placing flowers on my grave on cemetery day.

Who knows?

I ran into her good uncle the other day, and we reminisced about those days.

"Was up ta home last weekend," he said, "and ran into Sarah. Seems she never got over you leavin' and not returnin.'"

I didn't know that.

II

Bernie, the Midnight Movie Operator

A Story of Monsters and Love in Three Tales

9

Bernie, the Midnight Movie Operator

"He therefore turned to mankind only with regret. His cathedral was enough for him. It was peopled with marble figures of kings, saints and bishops who at least did not laugh in his face and looked at him with only tranquillity and benevolence...If anyone came upon him then would run away like a lover surprised during a serenade."
Victor Hugo—The Hunchback of Notre-Dame

Darkness can be a confederate for those who don't want to be seen. It allies with those whose deeds are primarily the concern of the law. It colludes with those whose faithfulness to another is all but gone. And it hides those who believe the world is better off not noticing them. Bernie considers himself one of the latter.

Born with a lazy eye and later marked by a severe case of acne, Bernie is also unusually skinny. Skinny like Twiggy skinny. In the darkness, Bernie feels safe. Darkness has become his mistress. He confides in her knowing she won't betray him to a world that embraces the lovely and abhors the freakish. Darkness protects him from the jeers and tears. It's the major reason Bernie became a midnight movie operator.

For the last twelve years, Bernie has been the projectionist at the

Florida Theater in downtown West Palm. He started in late September of 1960 and was trained under the watchful eye of old man Percy who learned his trade somewhere back north, people say. Percy began running films during the days of silent film actor Harold Lloyd, and, during the mid-20s, he moved to South Florida, worked for a time at the Palms Theater and then took a job as the projectionist across the street at the Florida Theater when it opened in 1949. Years later, while training his young protégé, Percy would often talk in reverence about those days of silent films. "The glory days of cinema" he would exclaim! And then he would lower his voice and talk about Lucy—Lucy Taliaferrio, the Palms Theater movie house organist. Lucy and Percy often met in the projection booth after the theater emptied to discuss a movie's plot. At least, that's what Percy told the manager one night when he interrupted the two and found Lucy flushed and her hair disheveled. Normally the manager would not have minded, since he often fantasized disheveling that hair himself; however, he felt it just wasn't right with Percy. You see, Percy was black, and Lucy was white. That night Percy disappeared for over two weeks. When he later returned to his job in the projection booth, he had a noticeable limp. Percy said he fell off the outside stairs leading up from the alley and broke his leg. Soon after that night, Lucy also left for Tallahassee and moved in with her sister. She later became a church organist, and some say, after a respectable length of time, ran away with the choir director to Alabama. They had six children. Percy never saw her again.

Bernie had applied to the Florida one night after watching the premiere of Alfred Hitchcock's *Psycho*. He noticed a small card in the ticket window—Help Wanted, Projection Assistant. The card was hand-printed by Percy. Percy was always proud of the fact that he could read and write. He hired Bernie on the spot because he felt Bernie had an aptitude for working in the dark. Bernie said his whole life trained him for darkness.

On his application, Bernie gave the Hotel George Washington as his address, although he didn't actually live in any of the 160 rooms. One night while wandering, looking for shelter during a rainstorm, he happened upon an unlocked window in the alley to the lower level of the hotel. Crawling quietly into the darkness, he was able to find a damp, stank corner that was not covered in water, and, with the help of some old forgotten towels which had the monogram HGW sewed in large scrolled letters in the middle of one end, he weathered the night. Returning there night after night, he soon realized no one ever came to that part of the building. There were no lights either. Since most of the floor held water when it rained, Bernie figured that the staff had abandoned this part of the hotel. So, he made a wall of boxes that were filled with items no longer used and cornered off a place to sleep. He left the smallest of cracks for him to slip through—the advantage of being skinny. Setting up an old mattress on some shipping pallets to keep him out of the water when it rained and adding a few orange crates as furniture, he called it home. Bernie never minded the rats. They liked the darkness too.

Four years later Percy died and was buried in Evergreen Cemetery. The cemetery was for blacks only. No one but Bernie and an elderly white woman attended. After the funeral, the lady introduced herself as Lucy. She didn't give Bernie her last name.

Management gave Bernie the weekend midnight movie schedule for Friday and Saturday nights. The crowd was made up of midnight movie vampires who only pretended to need the night. The movie vampires were teenagers, stoners, and couples who were looking for a dark place to rendezvous for an hour or two. Bernie would watch silently from his dark booth above and fantasize he was among the daylight crowd. He longed for a physical visage that would allow him to have a rendezvous. Especially with her—his lady in the yellow dress.

Every Saturday night his beautifully mysterious lady in the yellow dress would appear in the second row from the back, three seats in, alone, eating a small popcorn. Bernie had never seen her face; she always came in while he was setting the movie up and left while he was busy with the take-up reel. It was never a problem for her to get the same seat since most of the midnight crowd were territorial and sat near the front, leaving her to herself. Bernie respected her need to sit alone in the darkness.

Percy had said that learning the art of running a movie projector was not that hard if you had good timing. It's all about the timing, he would declare to the eager young apprentice. Bernie took to it quicker than most. The Florida Theater had a two-projector setup. Each projector had a two-reel system. One reel held the film while the other worked as a take-up reel. The trick was starting the other projector at the precise moment so the audience never knew the film was on two or more reels. On Friday's showing, Bernie would arrive early so he could inspect the film for any damage. He then ensured the leaders and tails of each reel were spliced correctly, and the cues were in their proper place. Most patrons never notice the cue dots in the upper-right corner of the picture screen, but to the trained eye of the projectionist, recognizing the dots was crucial for the seamless showing of multiple reels. Percy said "'dat pock-face kid" was the best he'd ever seen when it came to working film.

One Saturday night while prepping, Bernie heard someone crying softly below his booth. Looking down, he saw it was his lady in yellow. Slipping down the stairs and remaining in the shadows behind her, Bernie quietly and gently asked if there was anything he could do to help. He longed to reach out to her and take her in his arms and hold her until all her tears were dry. But all he dared do was offer verbal assistance. Without turning around, the lady sobbed, "No, there's nothing you can do. I just want to be left alone. Please." As he turned to go, he heard her whisper, "Thank you. You're very kind."

She spoke! He had heard her speak, and she said that he was kind! This was a day in Bernie's life that he would immortalize. The moment when she, the lady in yellow, *his* lady in yellow, said he was "very kind." The sound of her voice had him spinning as he climbed the stairs back to his dark booth. Her voice, he knew from now on, would be the last memory he would replay each night as he drifted off to sleep. The memory would greet him each day as he woke. The words, "You're very kind" almost convinced Bernie that he was a part of the daytime crowd with no need to remain in the shadows. He knew that the love he had for her was of his own manufacturing, but it was the only love he had ever experienced. No one ever in his life had said he was kind. Why his own mother often called him ugly, and she never threw him a birthday party with all the neighborhood children, and balloons, and a pony to ride. In fact, she rarely acknowledged that day except for when she needed him to watch his younger brother while she went out with someone who was not his father. His own father never acknowledged that day either. He would have had to come around to do that. But his lady in yellow, she said he was kind, and she didn't just say kind, but "you're very kind."

That night's showing was the 1970 film *Zabriskie's Point*. When it came to the scene where the main characters made love, Bernie imagined it was he and his lady in yellow. He pretended they were the ones rolling around in the desert naked and covered in dust. He believed that after making love over and over to his lady in yellow, he would hold her in his arms and cry. In the darkness of the projection booth, he actually was crying. He was crying because he had never made love to a woman before, and he often believed he never would.

After that night, his lady in yellow never returned to the midnight movie.

The following Friday, Bernie came to the manager's office to pick up the film, which generally was already placed in the projectionist's booth. The manager was in a rage about some new counter girl who had violated theater policy and added three shots of chemical butter to the popcorn instead of the usual two shots. He said the midnight movie vampires didn't pay the usual price for these late showings, so they shouldn't be given any special treatment. Popcorn, drinks, and candy were how the theater made up the difference in the lower midnight ticket costs. Bernie just happened to catch the manager's eye and at the same time his ire for some insignificant thing that really had nothing to do with Bernie's responsibilities. He figured the manager was just venting again about his marriage that everyone knew was full of unfaithfulness. His wife was so brazen that she even came to a midnight movie with her current love interest. They were both so drunk that she had not noticed they were at the Florida Theater. But tonight, Bernie sensed there was something else bothering the manager. The fat kid that worked the candy counter signaled him over, and in a whisper, he asked, "Did you hear about that woman they found dead in the alley dumpster last night?"

Keeping his head lowered and his cap pulled down so the fat kid couldn't clearly see his face, Bernie replied he knew nothing about it, and the fat counter kid said he was surprised since "it was last Saturday night after your shift."

Sudden panic and fear seized Bernie, and he grabbed the candy counter to steady himself, and his head began to spin, and his stomach began to tighten. "Do they know who . . . who she was . . . do . . . do they know who did . . . who did it?" Bernie stuttered.

"No, they ain't caught the guy yet. Some figure it could of been one of the midnight vampires, but I ain't heard nobody say for sure yet. The lady ain't been identified 'cuz her face was so beaten in that the cops say they may never know who she was."

The fat kid was still talking when Bernie let go of the counter and started slowly for his booth with his film canisters.

"The manager is all upset 'cuz the cops say she had a ticket stub for *Zabriskie's Point* on her. She must have been here 'fore she got killed. The only thing I hear that the cops got is that she was wearing a yellow dress."

Film canisters suddenly hit the floor with a loud bang, and one of the reels opened and began to roll unreeling yards and yards of celluloid into the lobby. The manager came running out of his office to see what the commotion was all about just as Bernie ran past him out of the theater and into the street blinded by his tears and holding his stomach while it tightened into nausea. He ran through the midnight crowd into the darkness until it swallowed him in an alley. Leaning against the alley wall, Bernie gave in to the nausea. He leaned over and retched until every muscle and joint in his body ached. His head began to spin again as he tried to focus through his tears. And as the convulsions in his body began to lessen, he suddenly became aware that some of the midnight vampires had followed him into the alley. Turning slowly and wiping his mouth with his sleeve, Bernie pushed through the small crowd and headed back to the theater. He was determined to find out who did this unspeakable thing to his lady in yellow, but for now, he just wanted to get back to his sanctuary of darkness in his booth. Tomorrow, he vowed he would find the person responsible. But for tonight, he wept.

Bernie's plan was to hang out on the fringes of the midnight crowd as often as he could to see if anyone said anything about the killing. He would set up his film early and then run down and out into the street to listen. Later while the film was showing, he would slip down and sit behind the crowd to listen again. And after the film, Bernie would run out and follow the crowd and listen and then later return to his booth to rewind the film.

The next night outside the theater, Bernie overheard a midnight movie vampire bragging about watching the killing to two others.

"Yeah, that chick really screamed. She was a fighter, but ol' Vince shut her up," he told the others.

Using the darkness, Bernie followed him as he walked along with the two others. When the three separated, Bernie overtook the dark pretender and walked alongside with naturally slumped shoulders and his cap pulled down low.

Bernie mumbled, "So, you seen that lady get killed?"

Without suspecting because he was high on speed, the movie vampire's youthful insanity began to brag, "Yeah, man, the chick was raisin' hell. You know, screamin' and kickin' and everything. It was Vince who got real rough and killed her after she refused to party at his place. I held her while Vince raped her, then he beat her, and choked her 'cause she wouldn't stop screamin'.'"

Holding his rage, Bernie pushed his hands deep into his pockets as his eyes scanned the alley for an instrument. The talkative dark pretender never saw the pipe that cracked open his skull or felt the warm blood as it spilled onto the alley floor. He never heard the words, "You son of a bitch!"

Two days later, Bernie heard the police found a dead movie vampire in an alleyway dumpster.

The next weekend Bernie came early to his shift. Dripping from the rain that had soaked him as he sprinted in from the alley back door, Bernie made his way to the lobby avoiding the manager and asked the fat candy counter kid, "Hey could you point out Vince when you see him."

Bernie waited in the shadows behind a free-standing movie poster advertising the next coming attraction. The fat kid nodded to Bernie when Vince came in with a bunch of movie vampires, and Bernie turned and headed to his upstairs booth. His hands trembled as he threaded the film. He was so anxious that for the first time, he almost missed the cue dots when it was time to change reels. Leaving the rewinding of the film for later, Bernie quietly followed Vince when he left the lobby and headed down an alley with several movie vampires in tow. The rain was falling harder now as they raced through the alley to some shelter. Bernie kept far enough back using the darkness to hide himself. Darkness and Bernie often worked together. Turning down another alley, the group bounded up a fire escape stairway to an unlocked window on the third-floor landing. Bernie crouched next to some broken wooden crates that someone had been busting up on the alley floor and waited. He absently picked up a piece and noticed a hammer lying next to it.

When the lights went out, Bernie waited for that unconscious hour when sounds are dreams. Carefully climbing the fire escape stairs to the still unlocked window, Bernie slipped into the dark apartment. Searching through the sleeping bodies, he found Vince in a bedroom with some underage midnight movie vampire initiate. No longer shaking, Bernie gripped the wooden stake in one hand and the hammer in the other. The underage girl never heard Vince's moan or the sound of escaping air.

No white person had ever been buried at Evergreen Cemetery. The arrangements for the burial were made by an elderly lady who used the name—Lucy Taliaferrio. His lady in yellow was laid to rest next to Percy. Only Bernie and Lucy attended.

10

The Fairies Aren't Coming

H*ere, thou incestuous, murderous, damned Dane, Drink off this potion. Is thy union here? Follow my mother.*
Hamlet—Act V, scene ii

Slipping back out the window onto the fire escape, the skinny young man grabbed the handrail and leaning over the side threw up into the alley below. He dropped the hammer he was carrying and then holding his hands up to the pouring rain as if he was worshipping a higher power, he let the rain rinse the blood from his hands. Quietly he made his way down the ladder to the alley below and then disappeared into what was left of the night.

Killing a midnight movie vampire has the possibility of altering one's psyche permanently, but Bernie grew somewhat indifferent over a short period of time. He justified his actions because the movie vampire had taken the only one Bernie had believed he truly loved. Bernie had experienced a long time ago that sometimes killing is how you express your anger with a world that rejects you or rejects the one whom you think you love even if that one doesn't love you back. Bernie developed this philosophy soon after his stepdad killed his mother. Not that she didn't need killing, he often thought, because of the way she treated him. And he certainly agreed that the absence of her life in this world did not mar the universe one iota; it certainly improved his life. But his was a world of darkness. Not just the darkness as in the absence of light, but the darkness of the soul. This darkness perverted his understanding of what is right and what is wrong. The darkness led him to decide that wrong was sometimes right—like killing his stepdad.

Climbing through the window of his basement hideaway, Bernie's thin frame slipped easily between the wall and the cardboard boxes he had stacked so as not to be detected by any wandering hotel personnel. His eyes quickly adjusted to the dark, dank basement. He felt and heard the many rats scurrying to avoid their non-threating roommate. Bernie sank down to his makeshift mattress and silently prayed the sleep that so often blackmailed him would come in this hour without its usual ransom in nightmares. Living his life was hard enough, Bernie thought. But reliving it night after night was hell. Truth is, hell was probably less horrific than this world of abstract visions and images that assaulted him in the form of monsters. He lay there as the imagined sound of scratching fingernails on concrete began. The monsters were crawling toward him, and they were dragging the memories of bloody bodies with them.

Memories! Monsters! If only these monsters had been destroyed when he was still a child. Most parents shoo away the monsters of bad dreams with their love and protection at the end of a child's day. They wage battle with reminders of times when childhood is full of excitements and pleasures. If only he could convince the monsters that his reality did not have to be. If only . . . if only his mother had loved the monsters away. Tossing back and forth in his bed like a child with a fever, Bernie tried to pretend that his mother would soon enter and wipe his fevered brow with a cool cloth and gently reassure him that the monsters would not come tonight. But it was hopeless. They kept scratching and creeping forward, whispering, hissing for him to release his mind to their dark thoughts. They clawed their way up his bed, rubbed calloused fingers over his face, and whispered with the stench of rotting corpses into his ears—sleep . . . sleep . . . dreeeam.

. . . Shhh, come follow me to the closet, sweet brother. No, no, don't worry about the shouting. I'll protect you. Quiet now; don't cry; they'll hear you. Shhhh, remember our game. We must stay quiet if we want the fairies to carry us away to their beautiful place. Shhhh, my sweet baby brother. Stay here while I make sure all is ok. Remember not a sound or the fairies will not come. I will come back for you when it is safe. I'll just creep along the floor in the dark. Remember, the darkness is our friend. I'll just see if he's gone. What's this! Why is this floor so warm and so sticky? Why is he kneeling over her? Why is she lying so still? Mommy! MOMMY! GET OFF HER YOU BASTARD, OR SO HELP ME I'LL . . . .

Jerking upright quickly, the monsters still whirling all around him and trying to regain their hold, Bernie's scream scattered the bed rats. Reaching out in the darkness and falling to the floor, he realized he had been dragged again into those memories that reminded him his own deeds were judged by others as no less evil than the crimes committed against him. Sitting there on the floor, he slowly became aware that his nightmares were creeping back into his world and would simply wait for another opportunity to pounce again. Lifting himself up, Bernie went slowly over to the basin of water, washed his face, and, running his fingers through his hair, imagined what the outside world would see. He had no mirror; in this light or absence thereof, one couldn't see anyway. His shirt was soaked in nightmare sweat, and there were traces of blood from Vince, so he changed into one that was less damp and had less odor. He needed to get rid of the shirt, but it would have to wait until after work. He slipped through the tight opening, and, as he emerged from his basement window into the alley, he noticed the bank's clock tower shining in the evening's darkness. He was late for work, so Bernie sprinted down the alley to the back of the theater and bounded quickly up the fire-escape stairs that led to his other sanctuary.

The manager had left the reels of film on the desk as he did every evening for the projectionists. Bernie quickly inspected the reels and began to thread the first reel with experienced fingers that flew over the celluloid through the various sprockets and return reels. A knock at the door startled him. He turned, looking over his shoulder to see the fat counter-kid, Clark, coming in with red flushed cheeks from climbing the stairs to Bernie's dark domain. From his sanctuary, Bernie's fantasies spilled out for when he needed something other than reality for a moment or two. Few ever came in and bothered him. The courteous knock was a long-ago practice that Bernie's late tutor, Percy, had imposed on all who might come in unannounced.

"Sorry to bother you, Bernie, but some guy was here earlier looking for you. He was some kind of cop in a suit. Left you this card," Clark said as he nervously handed the card to Bernie. Clark was always a little bit afraid of the reclusive projectionist and being here in the darkness with Bernie made his apprehension grow.

Taking the card slowly, Bernie looked at it while an icy memory began to scratch its way up his spine. On the front of the card, he read "Detective Delvecchio" with his phone number under the name. Turning the card over, he found the backside was blank. That was all the card revealed about the unexpected visit. Yet somehow that name seemed to invoke some distant memory in Bernie. The fat-counter kid suddenly brought Bernie back to the moment by asking, "Think it's kinda important? Maybe they want to talk to you about that murdered girl they found in the alley the other night. Huh, Bernie?" Looking around the dimly lit room, Clark commented, "Geez, man, you sure got a lot of equipment in here. Maybe someday you could show me how to run a film. I sure would love to . . . ."

"Thanks, I got to get back to work," Bernie said as he pushed the fat kid back through the door and locked it. His head began to swim, and he leaned against the door, trying to imagine what the detective could possibly want. Was it about the dead midnight movie vampire? Did he leave some evidence behind? He was so careful not to. But they had come to see him. Why? Maybe it was the mallet he dropped in the alley. Did they find some fingerprints on it? He assumed the rain would wash away any fingerprints. Maybe someone saw him climbing in or climbing out of the window. He had been so careful, yet they were here looking for him. Bernie reminded himself of his responsibilities and moved gracefully through the darkness to his projectors. Just as he was about to start the midnight feature, another knock made him jump. Cussing, he yelled at the locked door, "Damn it, Clark, I got to start the feature. Go away!"

"Sorry to interrupt, but this is Detective Delvecchio. I need to speak to the projectionist, Bernie. Would you please unlock the door?"

Detective Delvecchio here! Why was he here and so late? What could he possibly want? Turning and with a trembling hand, Bernie opened the door and stared into the eyes of a distant memory. Although the hair was now gray, the face was the face of the detective who many years ago investigated the murders of his mother and stepdad. Studying the pock-marked face of the projectionist, the detective slowly smiled and said, "Bernie! Do you remember me from a while back? I was the lead detective working the case on your parents' deaths. What's it been ten years, no . . . must be more than twenty since that time. How's your brother these days? I haven't heard from either of you since that nasty time. It's good to see you again and all grown up, workin' and runnin' things. This is great! Where did you disappear to? I lost track after the foster home took you in."

Lowering his head to hide his eyes under the bill of his cap, Bernie whispered, "Detective Delvecchio. What do you want with me?"

"Well, let's get right to the point. Ya see, the other night we found a young girl murdered, and she had a ticket stub for the midnight movie here," Delvecchio said as he pointed with his right index finger at the floor of the projectionist booth. "I know that you were the projectionist that night, and I was wondering if you happen to remember seeing her that evenin'? She was an attractive girl about your age, maybe a little older, and she was wearin' a yellow dress. You remember seein' someone matchin' that description?"

Bernie had to think quickly. He felt the detective was baiting him and Delvecchio already knew that he was the projectionist that night. What else did he know? Would telling him he knew her implicate him? Should he lie?

"So, Bernie, did you see the girl that night or any other night?"

Without looking up and risking the detective seeing the pain in his eyes, Bernie whispered again, "Yeah, I seen her. She would often come to the midnight showings, but I ain't seen her since that night here. Do they know . . . do they know who . . . who did it?"

"We got some leads. There was another murder last night near the same place in the alley. We think they might be related. You use the alley to come and go, you see anything unusual last night?"

Bernie quickly froze at the idea that Delvecchio knew he came and went by way of the alley. Had he been watching? Did he know where he stayed? What if he searched his make-shift room and found the blood-stained shirt? Or maybe he already had. But before he could respond, the jeers of the crowd below were shouting for the movie to start. Bernie jumped at the sound and then turned toward the cameras.

"I really need to get the film going. Could we do this later?" Bernie asked over his shoulder.

"Sure. I'll come by your place when you get off work. What's your address nowadays?"

Thinking quickly again, Bernie responded without turning around, "Perhaps I can meet you at the coffee shop on the corner . . . say, ten o'clock in the morning." He needed to keep the detective away from his place in case he *didn't* know where he lived.

"Ten o'clock at the coffee shop on the corner. I'll be there." Turning to go, Delvecchio stopped and over his shoulder said, "You know, we never did catch that guy you said broke in and killed your folks. It's interestin', I swear all the evidence indicated that your stepfather killed your mom, but we never found the guy what killed him." Turning back and facing Bernie, he continued, "We never found any evidence of forced entry. I remember your brother said it was monsters. Hah, monsters. The imagination some kids have. You remember any monsters, Bernie?" Delvecchio asked while laughing to himself and shaking his head slowly from side to side. "Monsters, humph. Some kids."

Stepping over to Bernie and bending at the waist to look up under Bernie's cap, Delvecchio searched for any sign of emotion out of this strange kid. He knew Bernie and his brother had it rough. Hell, there were enough 9-1-1 calls to convince him that Bernie's stepfather was no saint, no siree, but somebody did kill the man. And that somebody was pretty angry, filled with pent-up rage a psychologist would say. The force and violence with which he had been hit from behind knocked half his skull across the room. Delvecchio remembered the mess. He remembered the wide-eyed trauma in Bernie's younger brother.

At the door, Delvecchio hesitated before reaching for the door handle, saying, "Well, gotta go. See you tomorrow at ten at the coffee shop. Say hello to your brother. Sure would like to see him again."

"He's dead. He was killed in a hit and run two years ago."

Again over his shoulder, Delvecchio said in a tired voice, "Sorry to hear that. . . . Guess he's finally rid of his monsters."

When the door shut, Bernie finally let out his breath. He slowly dropped to the floor as *his* monsters rioted around him with memories of that night so long ago. He remembered the sound of the ball-bat shattering the back of his stepdad's head. He remembered the blood pouring out onto the floor, mixing with his mother's own blood. His monsters clawed their way into his memories, showing him images of himself pulling the dead body off his mother. He remembered the sickening wail coming from the hallway. That cry! That mournful cry! That cry . . . that sound of losing forever love's possibility as it mixed with death's blood. His baby brother, eyes wide with terror, stood in the doorway; from that moment forward, Bernie saw him forever silently screaming for his mother. Bernie remembered because his monsters would not let him forget.

At exactly ten, according to the bank tower clock, Bernie walked into the coffee shop. Delvecchio was already there sitting at the back, and he waved Bernie over.

"Prompt. I like that. Most kids nowadays don't respect the clock. How'd the movie turn out last night? Did they get the bad guy? Most times they do," he said, looking up with a smirk sipping his coffee.

Bernie didn't respond immediately. He just sat and stared down at his coffee cup, trying to figure out how much Delvecchio already knew and how to not give away any more information that could tie him to the murders. He knew Delvecchio hadn't bought the whole idea of an intruder all those years ago, but he seemed genuinely concerned for Bernie and his brother that night. He said he had kids of his own, and no kid should have to see their parents like that. No kids. Bernie figured Delvecchio saw the bruises on both the boys and put two and two together. He heard Delvecchio whisper to one of the officers' that he thought the stepfather deserved what he got. But today Delvecchio's sympathies seemed to be fading. He was pushing for what he thought Bernie knew. Hell, he might even put two and two together again.

"So, let's see. Where were we last night? Oh, yeah. Did you remember seein' anyone in the alley that night as you were comin' or goin'?" Leaning across the table and looking up under Bernie's ball cap at

Bernie's eyes, he asked, "Anything you tell me, anything at all is going to help me solve this case. You see, this guy that got killed he weren't no saint, and I figure he's the guy what killed that girl, but folks just can't go around killin' folks 'cause they got some sort of grievance against them. So, Bernie . . . did you see anything?"

Bernie raised his head slowly and looked Delvecchio in the eyes for a moment. Then he lowered his head back down and whispered, "No, I didn't see anything that night."

And then Delvecchio did what Bernie never imagined. He stood up and laid a couple of bucks on the table for the coffee. With one hand on the back of the booth and the other in front of Bernie on the table, he leaned down and whispered into Bernie's ear, "No girl should have to go through what that girl went through. No girl. The guy got what he deserved."

Delvecchio stood and rested his hand on Bernie's shoulder. "I'll be seeing you. You take care, you hear?" He paused. "Damn shame about your brother, Bernie. Damn shame."

11

Drowning Monsters

J ustice thunders, hungry for retribution. *"Stroke for bloody stroke be paid. The one who acts must suffer."*
Chorus—*The Libation Bearers*

"Delvecchio, you tightened the screws on that projectionist kid yet? Thought you said you had him. Come on, partner, what gives? You goin' soft again?"

Delvecchio looked up from the paperwork scattered across his desk at Hardy, his by-the-book partner. What was his excuse going to be this time? How could he hide the fact that the investigation was leaning toward Bernie as the one who killed that *scumbag* Vince, and he probably was the one who killed that other *scumbag* they found in the dumpster? He knew he was getting a reputation for not closing cases, and few wanted to work with him anymore.But, damn it, the way Delvecchio saw it, the creeps deserved what they got. Everyone knew the courts weren't doin' their job anymore. The creeps were walkin' 'cause of some so-called trauma they claimed in their past. Trauma my ass, he thought! What about the trauma the victims went through?

Still, in the back of his mind, Delvecchio knew folks couldn't just go around and whack people 'cause they don't like the court's judgment. He believed this, and the fact was weighing on him more and more these days. He knew he should close this case no matter what his conscience said. It was not right to let the skinny kid go. After all, what if someone pissed that kid off again? Delvecchio knew enough to know that if that happened, someone else would die.

He thought back to how long it had been since *that* case. How long had it been since, as Hardy says, he went soft? Just how long had it been since his wife couldn't live with him anymore? And, how long had he been ending every shift at the bar? He used to be like Hardy—by the book! But, when that drunk asshole ran down that poor kid and dragged him for four blocks screamin' all the while, Delvecchio changed. And the creep got nuthin'! He got nuthin' but time served. Claimed he had some trauma, some made-up trauma from his past that made him drink. And the jury bought it! Delvecchio remembered that night in the alley when he ran across that creep. He remembered when he pulled his service revolver, and, claiming self-defense, he shot four times, ending the sonofabitch what killed that boy. He wanted to believe he saw the bastard going for a weapon. Yeah, it was dark. Yeah, it was rainy. And yeah, the courts exonerated him even though no weapon was ever found on the victim. His own department said he did the right thing. Why even Hardy agreed it was a justifiable shooting when the perpetrator *supposedly* has a weapon. But, since that night, his sleep had tortured him. He'd see monsters. Hell, many would say *he* was a monster! And now, he's chasing a new one, a skinny, pock-mark faced kid who works as a midnight movie operator.

Bernie woke in his dark hotel basement refuge to the sound of the daily south Florida rain shower. That's what you get when you live in the tropics, he thought. It will shower at least once a day. Folks are used to it. They say it's good for the oranges. As he threw back the worn, mildew-smelling blanket, the rats scattered for the darker corners that even Bernie could not see into. He knew that today would be hard, so hard, but he needed to do this. The funeral was today—the funeral of the lady in the yellow dress. His lady in the yellow dress. The one that Vince violently took from him. The one Bernie wanted to believe could've brought light into all his darkness.

He stumbled over to the water bowl to wake up his face. Then he gathered his latest Goodwill clothes and crawled out of the alley window to head for the filling station bathroom to bathe and wash those clothes. The cemetery was a few miles from the station, and with body heat and a little breeze, his clothes would be dry by the time he arrived. Besides, he wanted to arrive early enough to find a place to observe without being observed. He didn't need Delvecchio finding him at the girl's funeral. Delvecchio was putting the pieces together. Seeing Bernie at the funeral would certainly give him another piece.

Hiding behind the large trunk of a Sable palm—it's easy for someone so skinny—Bernie listened as the black preacher said pleasant words over someone he did not know in an attempt to soothe the only one visibly present for his lady in yellow's funeral. The preacher silently marveled over the fact that this was the first white person he had ever officiated over and the first white person ever buried in Evergreen cemetery. At least, the funeral home had said they thought she was white. The lady who attended was white, and she looked familiar to Bernie. But from his vantage point, he couldn't clearly see her face in the shadow of her dark hat. As she glanced at the stone next to the freshly dug grave, Bernie stood erect in the palm's shadow. It was Percy's grave! His lady in yellow was laid to rest next to his old mentor. Now he remembered the lady. The last time he saw her was at Percy's funeral. It was Lucy! Percy's one love! Why was this girl being buried next to Percy? Unless? Could it be?

After the preacher left Lucy standing alone, staring down at the earth's dark open mouth, Bernie quietly and cautiously stepped out of his hiding and made his way toward her. Glancing from side-to-side and behind, Bernie kept an eye out for Delvecchio. He always had a way of showing up when Bernie least expected him. Approaching silently with his head down and his cap in his hands, Bernie whispered, "Excuse me, Lucy?"

Slowly turning to the skinny young man, Lucy smiled slightly at a familiar face. "Bernie, isn't it? You were Percy's apprentice. We met here years ago. It's good to see you again."

Bernie raised his eyes for just a moment to see the genuine smile coming from this mysterious lady he had only met once. He quickly lowered them again as he put his cap on and pulled it down to shadow his face from the world. "Yes, Ma'am, good to see you again. Did you, uh . . . did, uh, you know this lady?" Bernie stuttered as he tipped his head toward the grave.

Taking his arm and leading him over to a bench nearby, Lucy smiled with tears in her eyes as she said, "Elaine. Her name was Elaine. And yes, I did know her. She was my daughter."

Bernie stopped and raised his head to look at Lucy, "Your daughter?" Then after a slight pause, "Is she the part of the story that Percy never told me?"

Sitting heavily on the bench, Lucy smiled as she glanced back at the graves and then patted the bench seat next to her, "Sit with me a while, Bernie."

Bernie slowly sat with his hands folded together and hanging between his legs. He stared at the ground between them and waited for Lucy to continue.

"Yes, Elaine was the love Percy and I shared. Folks said it was wrong then. The world couldn't let love be love, so I had to leave, and Percy never knew his daughter." Looking again toward the graves, she continued in a lowered voice, "But now they are finally together. Now Percy has his Elaine in a place where love can be love." Looking back at Bernie, she asked, "But why are you here? Did you know Elaine? Did you meet her at the movie house? I know she went there a lot by herself to find a connection to her father. Did you meet her there?"

"Yes, I, uh . . . I, uh, saw her there often for the midnight showings. We only spoke once the night she was, uh . . . ," Bernie stopped. He turned his lowered head. Looking up from under his cap, he searched her face to see if she knew how his lady in yellow, Elaine, had died. He could see by the tears in her eyes she knew. He turned his head back and again stared at the ground between his legs.

Placing her hand on his arm, Lucy leaned her mouth close to Bernie's ear and whispered, "I know how she died."

She knew. But what did she really know? Did she know she was sitting on a bench next to the one who drove the stake into the heart of the midnight movie vampire? Did she know it was not the first time he had killed? He wondered if she knew about his monsters. Glancing again at her, Bernie longed to tell her. He needed to tell her, tell someone. He needed to be penitent. He believed until he did, his soul would never be absolved. Turning his face once again to the ground, he actually trembled as he confessed. "I'm, uh . . . I'm the one . . . I'm the one who killed that guy that hurt her."

Lucy's hand tightened on his arm, and then she slowly moved it away. Gazing up into the clouded blue sky, she thought for a moment before responding. "The world can be very mean to us sometimes, Bernie. It can be downright horrible, but that doesn't give us the excuse to be horrible back. The world was horrible to Percy and me. He never got the joy of knowing his daughter because of it. They beat him for loving me. But, Percy never fought back. He never fought back even though I wanted him too. I wanted him to destroy all the hate that existed in the world then, but he just held me tighter and loved all my anger away. He told me if we hated, we would never be strong enough to do what we had to do. He told me we had to let Elaine go and hide her in a world that did not understand love, real love. He told me if we hated, then Elaine would be hated. He couldn't allow that. So, we let her go." Looking back at Bernie, Lucy continued, "The people who raised Elaine were good people. They never knew the love that made her. They raised her blind to all the prejudice and all the evil in the world. They didn't know hate like I knew it at one time. I watched her grow from a distance, and when she became a beautiful young woman, I briefly came into her life. I told her of her father, Percy, and his extraordinary love and wisdom. I told her what he had told me—that hate destroys our hearts and our minds. It creates monsters."

When Lucy mentioned the monsters, Bernie studied her face and with fear in his eyes whispered, "I got monsters."

With sadness mixed with compassion, Lucy gazed into the face of the skinny, pock-mark faced kid while remembering Percy's strong arms of love around her, holding her, until the tears were for what would be and no longer for what was. She smiled, "Percy said we must drown our hate with our tears. Heavens! That man was so full of wisdom. Wisdom often comes when the world beats on you long enough. Percy taught me our sorrows were the only way to rid ourselves of the murder in our hearts." Pausing, Lucy took Bernie's hands in her own, and pierced his eyes with her own, "Bernie, don't let the monsters win. Hate makes them stronger. Weep—weep for love. It's the only way to be free. That's what Percy said."

Rising slowly to the lost future, Lucy began walking away but stopped. She smiled one more time at Bernie, whispering, "Remember to weep—weep for love." Then, she was gone.

"Interesting lady. Good advice gettin' rid of those monsters." The voice from behind startled Bernie, and he jumped up from the bench while turning to confirm who he already knew was there. Delvecchio stood there with a hard look on his face as if he were doing something that took a lot of effort. In his hand was a shirt—Bernie's shirt—and there was blood on it. Vince's blood.

Bernie couldn't decide whether to run or simply give up. Delvecchio had him or at least he had the shirt. He had left it in his basement shelter with the intent to get rid of it, but he forgot. Or maybe it was the rats? They might have dragged it out of sight into one of their darker corners. Bernie often thought they worked in league with the monsters. Regardless, Delvecchio had his final piece of the puzzle. He must have known all along where Bernie lived and searched his basement room when Bernie left this morning. Delvecchio just stood and studied the skinny kid as if he wasn't sure of his next move. A park bench stood between them, and if the kid decided to make a break, he wouldn't be able to stop him—not with all the living alone take-out dinners under his belt. The move was Bernie's.

"Listen, kid, I know life has crapped all over you and your brother, and then there's this girl. Not sure how she figures into it, but I know that you avenged her. I'm sure the creep deserved it. But, I'm bettin' the blood on this shirt will match that of the guy down in the morgue," Delvecchio said, holding the shirt up toward Bernie. "Revenge don't give you a pass. Not anymore. I can't let you walk this time. I gotta take you in. It's over. It's over for you, and it's probably over for me, too."

Bernie wasn't sure what Delvecchio meant by his last remark, but he could see the detective's eyes weren't certain about the next move. He glanced over Delvecchio's shoulder to the grave of the one he believed could have understood all his loneliness. Maybe she could have helped him weep for all the hate, but now he would never know. There was nothing left. So, he did what Delvecchio expected him to.

"Stop, kid! You can't run forever. I know about monsters. Eventually, they will pull you into a darkness you can't get out of. I can help! Let me help!" Delvecchio pleaded as the skinny kid disappeared beyond the gates of the cemetery. He shuddered at the memories of that night so long ago when Bernie's brother said there were monsters. He now realized that those monsters had been chasing Bernie most of his life. He knew Bernie would not survive them. Hell, he wasn't sure he could survive the ones that chased him.

Bernie made his way south down old A-1-A which ran along the coast. He hid from traffic from time to time in the scrub palmetto until darkness protected him and then made his way to the pier at Lake Worth beach. He hid among the pilings under the pier until the casual tourist crowd had left nothing but the local all-nighters, who with a sack full of fifteen-cent Royal Castle burgers and cartons of bait shrimp settled in for sunrise. Bernie made his way to the end of the pier.

Staring down into the darkness, he was aware of the repetitive sound of the high tide coming in. The waves slapped against the barnacle-covered legs that held the steady wooden platform high above the ocean floor. The spray of the waves felt cool on his face as he leaned dangerously far out over the waist-high railing. Just a little more and he could stop the voices now rising up inside him. A little more and all the hate would be drowned.

The monsters were clutching and grabbing at his shirt, pulling him farther and farther out over the rail. They tasted blood. His blood! The monsters didn't care who they killed as long as they could destroy. They needed Bernie's death before he could deny them. Before he stood against them. Before he wept for all the hate.

The next day a crowd had gathered at the end of the pier to watch the divers below carefully cut the skinny kid free from the net secured tightly to the pier just beneath the high tide. The net held the body in a crucified position. Later the divers said the body looked like it was at peace—like it gave into death willingly.

Delvecchio watched from above along with the crowd and whispered, "Damn shame. Damn shame."

III

Florida Tales and Other Wandering Stories

"Life is a succession of lessons which must be lived to be understood."
— *Ralph Waldo Emerson*

12

This Joker's Wild

Hooker's Point is a quiet, odd community here on the edge of the Loxahatchee River, named after Elijah Hooker, a Confederate soldier, who abandoned the war early and hid out in this mangrove swamp for years after General Lee had surrendered. He eventually began to eke out a meager living taking tourists by canoe upriver to see the battlefields of the Seminole Indian Wars. From this, he built a small quiet community of trade shacks, cabins, and chickee huts for the riverboat trade. The community remains quiet today mostly because there are not many who venture to the end of the shell-rock road off a two-lane blacktop.

The blacktop heads north to Jonathan Dickson State Park, a state park that has something for every member of the family. Families do not stop at Hooker's Point. Only locals who have fished here since their great-granddaddies told them of the spot know to turn left at the hand-painted sign hanging crooked by one nail from an old majestic giant bald cypress standing true, adorned with Spanish moss. Yeah, only the locals who love the quiet—quiet from all the yelling, fussing, splashing children and barking dogs on leashes and mothers looking for the perfect spot to set up the picnic in the shade and fathers hoping to catch some cute bathing suit sunning on the sugar sand beaches—come to Hooker's Point. The locals know they can always get fresh bait and a cold, cheap beer after the day's reflective and peaceful search among the dark waters. The locals know that once the tourists find out about this paradise at the end of this dead-end road, the quiet is over.

The community is odd because of the mixture of old and slightly less old buildings as well as the eccentric people and the slightly less eccentric people who live on this dead-end. A collection of rag-tag structures with a couple of old, worn docks stretch out into the tannin dark waters of the river. One neglected chickee from Elijah Hooker's day remains, leaning unsteadily to the west in the sawgrass. The other buildings are all arranged at the end of the shell rock road beginning with the garage/fix-it-shop run by Sanchez, a deep, ebony-black Vietnam vet. Sanchez claims—thanks to the United States government—he can fix anything from a toaster to a busted transmission on an M35 Deuce-and-a-Half. The shop is actually a WWII Quonset hut with a 1947 Airstream parked out back that keeps Sanchez out of the rain that comes almost daily at Hooker's Point. Next to the fix-it shop is a flat-roofed, cinder-block-walled hardware store that doubles as a post office and a parts depot for Sanchez. Next to the hardware store is an alleyway, roofed and closed at both ends to become a bait and tackle shop selling fishing supplies and Busch beer. The proprietor, an old blind man with gnarled hands from countless snake bites when he seines for minnows, rents flat-bottom boats when the locals want to fish upstream rather than from the bank or docks. And finally, there is a sun-weathered, cedar board-and-batten structure called the End of the Road bar.

The bar is aptly named because the road stops out front. Some say it is named for the collection of screwballs that live in this quiet community that call themselves the Violated Onions. The owner and bartender, ol' Doc Blanchard, referred to them as a bunch of rapscallions one night, and Sanchez, puzzling over the word's exact meaning, made a comment while clinching his cigar with his teeth, "You mean we's a bunch of violated onions." Strangely enough, it stuck.

Doc Blanchard lost his license to practice medicine because he lost a malpractice suit brought against him by his best friend's widow after Doc botched his surgery while drunk, killing his friend. The widow took everything Doc had and then some. Ironically, his best friend had left him this bar in his will, and Doc sleeps in the back storage room on an old Army cot Sanchez brought back from Vietnam. Doc also lost his wife and children because of his drinking, so now as penance every night, he drinks till he gets sick or passes out. He never wants to wake up happy again.

The two old docks creak and sway slightly from side to side, but those who come here are familiar with the movements and learned long ago not to overcorrect their balance. If you do, you could end up in the dark water with the gators who hang around below for the guts and scraps from the cleaning of the day's catch. One dock, the one with the fish cleaning table and water hose, holds the rag-tag collection of boats for rent that Sanchez keeps running for the old blind man with gnarled hands. Sanchez never cheats him though he says he certainly could since the old man cannot see the receipts for parts. "It just don't seem right," Sanchez would say, "to take advantage of him just because he cannot see to read." Most do not know that Sanchez cannot read past a third-grade level himself. Doc knows. He told Sanchez it's no one's *damn* business and keeps the secret between the two of them. Sanchez respects ol' Doc for that.

The other dock has a lone, dilapidated houseboat that lists a little to the starboard due to a hurricane that dumped water into one of the ballast tanks. The pump for that tank quit working at about the same time. Sanchez says he could fix it, but Jake—who lives there—says he likes it that way. He says it reminds him that everything in life is crooked and "there ain't nothin' anybody can do shit about it."

Jake, too, is a Vietnam vet. A Seminole Indian from the Tommy Tiger Cow Creek band, Jake was a former football star in high school. Everyone thought he would go on to play for the University of Florida Gators and then turn pro, but the conflict overseas took that from him. Unlike Sanchez, Jake claims not to have learned any skill "unless you call runnin' up smack a skill." Jake's habit is at times serious, and, if it were not for the efforts of Doc, Jake would probably have become another white cross in the old cemetery back down the shell-rock road.

The Violated Onions gather every Tuesday night at the End of the Road for their weekly poker game. Joining Sanchez, Doc, and Jake is Pete, a Baptist preacher on leave from his pulpit and his marriage because of an affair with his secretary. Pete is temporarily bunking with Jake on the houseboat. He sleeps on the port side because he is afraid the starboard side's leaning so close to the water's edge will allow some river monster to crawl in one night and drag him to the bottom of the black water. Jake says, "Just let 'em try." Pete's not so reckless. He worries his sins will cost him more than a marriage. He worries that God will use Nature as a way of punishing him. The truth is Pete punishes himself. Jake, Sanchez, and Pete all went to the same high school there in Jupiter, Florida, and they all played football together. Jake was the star running back, Sanchez played defense, and Pete mostly played the bench.

It was in high school that Pete met Ester, a missionary's daughter home on leave for her last year of high school. Pete and Ester were married two weeks after graduation because in Pete's words, "We defiled the marriage bed." He said marriage was their penance. Fourteen years later, he gave in to lust again and drove his secretary to the Motel 6. The problem now was that he was still married, and, according to the laws of the state, he could not marry away his sin to a second wife, at least not while he was still married to the first.

Soon after Pete's wife kicked him out and he moved in with Jake, Sanchez said to him, "See, I told you, Preacher, you Christians ain't none better than us what don't hold for that religion crap." Sanchez calls Pete Preacher to tease. He does, however, try his best not to cuss too much in front of Pete due to some teaching by his grandmother about respecting men of the cloth. Whenever he would let some curse word slip, he would apologize on behalf of his grandmother, and Pete would always say, "It's about our souls, not our mouths." Sanchez would just reply, "Bullshit!"

Sanchez and Pete always argue. Sanchez says he and Pete argue like an old married couple and do not take the arguing seriously except the one argument where Sanchez learned Pete sat out his time during the war as a conscientious objector. Pete said it was because of his religious convictions—he just "couldn't kill anybody." Sanchez says it was because he is a coward; Sanchez cannot forgive Pete for that.

Pete will not offer a response. Now one argument he will respond to is the one about his religious beliefs. Sanchez argues with Pete that "all them church folk are just a bunch of hypocrites." He loves to *rag* on Pete about this, but deep down inside he thought that maybe Pete was right about God. After all, there had to be a God, he thought. How else could you explain coming so close to death every day in Vietnam and somehow making it home in one piece? Yeah, there had to be a God. Sanchez just did not know who or what to call Him. Was He Jehovah? Was He Allah? Was He Buddha? Or was it just some higher consciousness that is in us? He didn't know. Until he did, he was not committing to anyone's idea, no matter how good a friend Pete was. Sanchez figured he would pick a god the moment before dying—that is if there was time. He hoped he would pick the right one.

When Sanchez walked into the bar on Tuesday night after a quick meal of rice and beans heated on the two-burner stove in the Airstream and an even quicker cold shower with a garden hose outback of the

Quonset hut, he noticed Doc with Jake and Pete huddled in one corner of the bar whispering.

"What's up, gentlemen? You meetin' to vote me out of the Onions or just strategizin' to beat me tonight at poker?" Sanchez said with his wide white smile while winking at Doc.

"Nah, just discussing the latest mess Jake here has gotten himself into. Looks like Big Bertha's got some more groceries for her meat locker," Doc said disgustedly as they all sat at the round card table set up near the bar opposite from the jukebox and the three-couple dance floor.

This mess of Jake's that Doc was referring to was not the first mess. All too often, Jake would resolve a person's conflict by *accidentally* killing the object of the person's problem. Jake has a way of reacting to situations that usually ended up with someone either getting seriously hurt or dead. To get rid of the evidence, Jake would throw the body in the swamp for the gators. The Onions all knew of Jake's reputation for reacting before thinking. When he reacted, the "gators got fed." Somewhere in the back of everyone's mind, they all believed the victims deserved Jake's retribution, which allowed them quickly to absolve Jake. But absolution had its consequences—knowledge made them accessories. Doc said whether the victims deserved it or not, Jake could not continue *reacting* when he felt threatened.

Now, Big Bertha was an old gator that hung out upriver at the long-deserted Trapper John's place. Some say that Trapper raised the gator from an egg, and it stayed protecting the place from unwanted visitors. Unfortunately, one of those unwanted visitors got past Bertha one black night and shot Trapper with his own shotgun. Rumor had it that Trapper had gold buried somewhere on his property there along the river, but none was ever known to be found other than the Mexican coins stuffed in his chimney.

"Man, who'd you go and kill this time, Jake? Did your smack dealer cut yur horse or did someone look at ya wrong at the K-mart?"

"It ain't funny, Sanchez. Leave him alone. We don't need Jake reacting again and feeding Bertha no dark meat," Doc sneered. Unlike Jake and Pete, Doc was not color blind. He liked Sanchez well enough, but sometimes his antiquated Southern prejudice just seeped out without any forethought.

Sanchez shot Doc a hurt look and wondered when Doc would, if ever, join the Civil Rights Movement and get past his prejudicial background. Sanchez picked up the cards and began to shuffle to give his mind something to do other than dwell on Doc's ignorance. As he threw the cards out around the table, Sanchez could no longer stand it any longer being the only one at the table who did not know what was going on.

Sanchez grumbled, "So, tell me . . . what's this here problem that everyone knows 'bout but me."

Doc looked down at his cards and began to shuffle them in his hand into a possible winning strategy. Everyone knew that Doc always arranged his cards to suggest that he had a good hand dealt to him. Most of the time, everyone knew it was a bluff. Continuing to look at his cards, Doc almost absentmindedly began to tell Sanchez of Jake's latest "reaction."

"It seems that Jake here was hired by an old flame to straighten out a problem she was having with her ol' man. Jake says he went over to lean on the guy and convince him to treat his wife right when the husband—who was drunk I might add," Doc said looking up at Sanchez to emphasize the evils of alcohol, "well, it seems the guy took a swing at Jake and you know Jake, well . . . he reacted. He punched the husband in the throat and crushed his windpipe, and the man choked to death right there in front of his wife."

Sanchez looked over at Jake, who kept his eyes on his cards, but Sanchez knew that Jake's Ranger training taught him to observe everything while looking at nothing.

"Jake, when you gonna learn that you cain't go 'round killin' other people's problems and feedin' 'em to ol' Bertha," Sanchez said in a best friend tone. Sanchez really believed most people had it coming and often wondered why he did not react more like Jake. They both had been to the same war. They both came home brutalized in their minds. They both had seen things that decent men should never see. Maybe the tendency to react came from Jake's heroin addiction. Sanchez always thought Jake was half the man he used to be because of that dope even though he still could take out most of the bar before Sanchez could get out of his seat. But he also knew that someday the law would catch up with Jake. Then, he thought of Detective Martin Buchanan, Jake's high school rival in football and women, who was always looking to bust Jake to even the score from so many years ago. It seems that whenever the two met on the field, Buchanan always walked away—the loser. He even lost his girlfriend, Audrey, to Jake the night of the prom. Buchanan showed up in a rented limo, but Audrey had already left in Jake's '68 road-stripe yellow Chevy van. Jake liked to brag that he actually had a waterbed in the back of the van—just in case. Buchanan went to the prom alone. He swore that someday he would get even with that "damned, red-skinned swamp stomper."

"You know Sanchez is right," Pete said, looking at Jake until Jake raised his eyes to meet Pete's, "You got to stop this. The war's over, and you can't make everyone your enemy nowadays. I know the war screwed you up and the heroin takes away your reason, but one day Buchanan's going to walk through that door," Pete said pointing to the front of the bar, "and haul you away. Think about it. You won't last one day locked up. Besides you don't get to decide who dies and who lives—that's God's job."

Sanchez started to challenge Pete, but Doc interrupted. Jake turned to Doc as he offered in a fatherly tone, "Listen to your friends, Jake. They're telling you the truth. This has got to stop before it's too late. You're getting as wild as this Joker that Sanchez didn't cull out." Doc peered over his glasses at Sanchez as if to say he knew what Sanchez was attempting.

Doc flipped the card at Sanchez and tapped his pile for another. Sanchez acted surprised that he missed that Joker but grinned, knowing the purposed move threw Doc off his game.

Poker night was always filled with usual habits like drinking whiskey and smoking cigarettes and cigars. Pete did not smoke and was always complaining about those that did. Doc's taste for finer things developed when he had his practice and his money. He enjoyed his vodka more than the others, so Sanchez always produced a bottle from somewhere. Jake thought someone owed Sanchez for some work he had done in the past, and Sanchez worked it out in trade. Doc did not need more alcohol, but Sanchez, for some reason, truly cared for Doc and always said to the others, "What's it gonna hurt?" Everyone else drank beer. The night looked to be promising except for that thing with Jake. There is always a *thing* with Jake.

"Any chance Buchanan can make the connection? You got that lady under control? By the way, who was it? Was it Sherry? I remember she had a thing for you," Sanchez said while studying Jake's face for some kind of reaction.

Jake stared at Sanchez.

"It was Sherry! I knew it! You done an' went an' killed her ol' man. Shit, Jake! Don't cha know that he's a cop or, should I say, was a cop. Buchanan is definitely comin' for you. Shit, man! Your ass is grass. I'm tellin' ya. Grass!" With an irritated voice, Sanchez flung his discards on to the table, all the while meeting Jake's stare with his own.

Sanchez never tip-toed around Jake. He would always tell him that he went through the same damn war, and it was time for Jake to "get over it!"

But Jake could not get over it. Not with his addiction. His reasoning and resolve were all but gone.

Getting Jake to talk about anything, especially anything that was a problem like his addiction or killing folks, was near impossible. They all knew that, so Sanchez decided to change the subject for now. He fully planned to come back to it after the game. But for now, he turned to Pete and said, "Hey thanks for sellin' me that shotgun, Preacher. It's pretty sweet! I named it Betty after the first girl that slipped me the tongue."

Everyone looked up and stared at Sanchez. Jake muttered with surprise under his breath to Sanchez, "Geez, Sanchez, didn't you date some girl named Betty last month?"

Sanchez grinned, "Yeah, that was her."

Jake laughed. Pete looked suspiciously at Sanchez, wondering why he would tell such an obvious lie. Sanchez winked at him and then nodded toward Jake. Jake continued to smile as he threw his discards and asked for two. Pete, without looking up, chuckled to himself understanding.

Now, Doc took great pride in the fact that he could shuffle the cards like a Vegas dealer. It ruffled Sanchez's feathers, and he often told Doc to just deal. He used strategies against Doc, and this was Doc's strategy against him. Doc knew if he irritated Sanchez, then Sanchez was more likely to make a mistake. Slowly he passed out the cards to each player. When he dealt to Sanchez, Doc appeared to accidentally throw two cards. He quickly grabbed one and put it back on the bottom of the deck.

Sanchez grinned and said to Doc, "Just deal out four or five, and then you pick the right ones to give me."

"Sorry, Sanchez. Jake's got me riled. You want I should deal over?"

"Just play the damn cards!"

The game ended around midnight, and everyone started for their beds. Doc was very drunk, so Sanchez helped him to his cot. Doc protested that he could manage and did not need "no help from no colored man."

"Why you always got to insult me with that colored shit. I'm just a man like you." Sanchez said, angry this time.

Doc stopped and studied Sanchez as if he was seeing him for the first time. He pondered over Sanchez's face through vodka-soaked eyes. Then lowering his head with alcoholic shame, he mumbled, "I truly am sorry, Sanchez. You know I love you like a son, and I truly don't mean what I say sometimes. Just write me off to bad raising."

"Doc, ain't no amount of bad raisin' excuses your damn southern racism. Like I always tell Jake—get over it!"

He gently lowered the old man to his cot and covered him up with a blanket. Doc had already passed out when Sanchez switched off the light.

The next morning Jake rose early as was his custom. Pete asked him once if it was his military training. Jake said no. He said he always got up before the sun to have time to be thankful for another day. He said his father taught him that. Pete nodded and agreed it was a good custom. He said he used to rise early to talk to God, but lately, he did not think God wanted to talk to him. Jake examined Pete and, for a moment, felt pity for the man who was once in tight with the Creator, but now could not be thankful for the morning.

Morning at Hooker's Point always began slowly. It began early, but slowly. Especially for Doc. He always stumbled from his cot to his coffee pot. His first cup included a shot of Jameson's to help him face the new day. Unlike Jake, Doc did not greet the day with thankfulness.

Sanchez, on the other hand, was neither thankful nor unthankful. He was just busy. If he did not have something to fix that produced income, he was working on his "baby." His baby was a faded black '67 GTO Judge. Sanchez had pulled the engine and transmission while the body stood empty over in the far corner of the shop covered with an old tarp. He planned to get to the body one day and deal with the rust around the bottom of the doors caused by exposure to the salt air.

While he was organizing for the day, Pete walked in and asked, "Whata we gonna do about Jake? We can't let him go on like this. One day Buchanan is gonna pull into the parking lot, and it's all over for Jake."

"Well, I ain't got no ideas, Preacher. That shit—sorry Grandma—that dope he puts in his arm got him all screwed up in the head. Maybe he needs to get caught. You know, just so he can see the mess he's made."

"You know Jake won't make it in prison. He'll kill himself tryin' to get out. We gotta find something to make him see that God doesn't like him goin' around killin' folks just 'cause he thinks it's somehow justified."

"Well, Preacher, maybe we should let *God* take him down," Sanchez said with some sarcasm. "Look at how He's fixed you."

Pete did not answer. He just gave Sanchez a hurt look. Sanchez was not sure if it was for his insensitive remark or because Pete knew it was true. Pete turned to leave and offered over his shoulder, "We gotta do something. We just got to!"

The week passed by without any more conversation about Jake. In fact, Jake was visibly absent from everyone. They all knew that he was holed up in his houseboat sticking a needle in his arm to chase away the demons of his latest reaction. Pete kept his distance. Sanchez, too. Doc, as usual, monitored Jake's descent, anticipating stepping in to rescue Jake from an early grave.

Tuesday came around, and the Onions slowly drifted in for the game—including Jake. Doc had intervened and pulled him back from his lone pilgrimage of destruction, back to the sober reality of the people who deeply cared for him. Sanchez, as always, was the last to arrive.

"Well, boys I need to pay for a carburetor, so let's open for a nickel," Sanchez said, smiling.

The cards were dealt.

"Let's make it a dime. Chase away the sanity," Doc offered as he threw in his ten-cent chip.

"Awful bold there, Doc," Pete remarked, throwing in his chip.

"Well, it's early, and I'm sober."

Sanchez looked up quickly and chuckling said, "Sober, huh. That's rare. Maybe now I can chase you out, again."

"The hell you will!" Doc responded, draining his glass of Vodka in one swallow.

"Sounds like sour grapes to me," Sanchez said, studying his cards.

Doc glared back at Sanchez, "Man, you ain't heard sour yet. I'm about to make Beaujolais. Read 'em and weep. Three Kings—the Magi!"

While Doc shuffled the cards, Sanchez took his cigar out of his mouth and used it as a pointer, "Jake, I been studyin' on this matter of you reacting, and I think I got me a solution. You need to take ol' Pete here," he said, pointing with his cigar, "with you when you got a client. Pete don't do no killin', so maybe he can keep you from doin' the same."

Pete knew Sanchez was taking another jab at the conscientious objector position he took during Vietnam. But he didn't respond. He just asked for two while staring at his cards.

"That's not a bad idea," said Doc as he nodded once in Sanchez's direction.

Sanchez knew that agreeing with him was Doc's way of saying he was sorry for his racial remarks the other night. Sanchez nodded back while clinching his cigar in a smile.

"Yeah, maybe I could use a little restraint," Jake laughed mostly to himself without looking up.

Everyone focused on Jake with disbelief. How could he take his dark actions so lightly? They returned to the game, and the mood slowly lifted. Sanchez was the first to chuckle, and then Doc joined in, laughing through tight lips, moving his shoulders up and down while keeping his eyes on his cards. Pete stared up at the ceiling, shaking his head from side to side, rolling his eyes, uttering, "Geez! We're all goin' to hell."

Sanchez noticed car lights pulling up outside and getting up walked over to the window. Over his shoulder, he quipped, "Well, lookie who's here?"

13

Cottonmouth Mather

T*hey shall take up serpents . . . it shall in no wise hurt them*
—Mark 16:18

From the nest high in a majestic cypress, the eagle could see the slow and barely noticeable bending of the grasses on the edge of the swamp even though the sun was setting. She was glad for the protection of this high perch for the hatchlings. They needed this haven until they were big enough to survive on their own. A swamp is a place where life and death exist together at the same time. She knew the movement instinctively below would not bring life.

Peering through her cat-eye pupils, the snake used the pits between her eyes and nostrils to detect every minute difference in temperature as she moved silently on her prey. The hunger in her belly was weeks old; the eggs in her were months old. She gave no thought to her hatchlings; she only thought of feeding herself. Something moved up ahead. The sun was all but gone as she silently moved closer to the source of heat. She would not strike until she was in perfect range for her deadly bite. It took weeks to replenish her venom so the hit had to be perfect because it would leave her defenseless. The prey would only resist for a moment.

Here—life brings death, and death brings life.

116

There is nothing more beautiful and nothing that brings more peril than fog at sunrise in the swamp. It adds mystery to the unseen danger that is hidden just below the surface or dangling from some tree branch. Large bald cypress with Spanish moss are like giant elders keeping watch over the tidewater flowing in and out from the river that stretches to the sea. The mangrove with its many-fingered roots sinks deep into the mud of the tannish water making up a false shoreline for the cranes and herons to use as a perch for their daily meals of crawdads and small fish. When the water lies still and glass-like, it creates the illusion of peace and tranquility. But below the surface near the pretend shoreline often lies a quicksand that welcomes a misstep from some unwary stranger. Its embrace holds you until exhaustion gives over to acceptance of a death not sought nor wanted. Giant reptiles share the waters too along with their many teeth and silent wakes. To the unfamiliar, they appear on the surface more like some fallen tree that is merely an obstacle to navigate around.

Life and death—thus is the way of the swamp.

The Seminole know best how to navigate the stillness with their cypress dugout canoes and long poles — soundlessly pushing through the dark waters. Even the black bears and black panthers are not disturbed. The Seminole belonged here in the swamp. Since the Indian Wars of the early to mid-1800s, they have lived fiercely independent lives while quietly at war with the country, passing on their way of life to their sons and their sons and their sons. They have learned to navigate the open sawgrass plains easily using the horizon as a marker, but once they enter into the hammocks and thickets, the horizon vanishes. All sense of direction is lost once inside the shadows. The channels, the lagoons, and the deep creeks meander forever—twisting and turning and tumbling over one another without warning.

This is where being born to the swamp takes over. Beginning life here means you're more likely to survive the swamp's challenges. Those who did not begin life in the swamp rarely tell tales without shuddering from the memory. Some never get the opportunity to tell tales. Only those who believe in something greater than luck or have an instinct from their heritage survive.

More life, more death—the way of the swamp.

But if you know the way through the hidden channels and are unafraid of the darkness and its deathly creatures you can find a walled hut with a single dock that began as a chickee deep in the swamps. Smoke drifts aimlessly from a small fire located in the corner of the deck of the chickee. The fire heats the day's food in a cast-iron pot, and the aroma pleases the man as he squats in front of it, stirring the contents listlessly with a hand-carved wooden cypress spoon. The spoon is the man's only utensil; the pot is his plate. He has one cup.

The anticipation of the day's only meal aroused the saliva within the man's mouth as he gazed out the only window into the fog of the swamp. He heard a fish slap the water, and he thought that it would have been a nice addition to the meal. It had been days since his pot of swamp cabbage and root vegetables had been graced with some flesh, and his belly ached for something more substantial to quiet its growl.

The days had become weeks, months, maybe longer, since the man had paddled his seventeen-foot aluminum canoe to this self-imposed prison deep in the shadows now surrounded by the fog. The quietness touched his memories as he reluctantly revisited the events that had brought him to this dark isolation void of human contact but selected for its constant reminder of death.

Slowly the voices within his memory began . . .

"WE ARE A FALLEN PEOPLE! We need to shed this earthly shade we exist in and embrace the holiness that is our destiny. We need to stand boldly and naked before our Creator and repent of the many sins that weigh us down and keep us from the fellowship of the One that spoke our being into this existence. Come forward and partake of His everlasting grace by holding high over your heads the serpent that brought us to shame. Let not your fear keep you from the faith that will release you! COME! COME AND TAKE HOLD OF YOUR SIN!"

Reaching into the black box, the preacher gently lifted the heavy rattlesnake as it began to resist being disturbed from its slumber. The snake coiled around the preacher's arm looking for an escape as it instinctively felt uncomfortable in his grasp. Flinging itself forward, the snake landed on the dirty concrete floor. The sudden coolness agitated the serpent, and it began to vibrate its tail with a sound that warned the many souls standing too close that escape was its only mission. Striking at any movement, the snake sank its fangs into the crowd. Once, twice, three times it bit and released its possibility of death. The last appendage belonged to a youth of barely three years holding onto his mother's hand. His scream broke the crowd's ecstatic utterances as they rushed for the exit of the front doors, pushing and shoving without regard for the bitten or the serpent.

Three parishioners remained on the floor moaning along with the swelling while the preacher looked on with horror. The young boy no longer screamed. He lay silent and stared back at the preacher with eyes that could not see the world he had just begun.

The serpent silently and without notice escaped out the door and into the swamp.

"MY GOD! OH, GREAT JEHOVAH, WHAT HAVE YOU DONE! WHY HAVE YOU ALLOWED THIS PUNISHMENT TO FALL UPON US?" the preacher yelled with clenched fists raised to heaven. Weeping, he kneeled beside the limp body of the young boy and cradled him in his arms, rocking back and forth. From way deep inside where true pain begins, the wailing rose to the surface. A wailing that was related to the wailing heard in the Garden so long ago. A wailing that could be heard far into the swamp as it echoed through the tangle and the voids.

The sound made no impression on this rattlesnake as he only thought of filling his long empty belly.

As the angry sound receded into the man's memory, the hissing of boiling stew climbing up and out of the pot and onto the fire brought him back to his present isolated torment. Although he tried hard to forget the guilt and pain, it seemed somehow it was a necessary part of his penance. Tears welled up in his eyes.

How many times would he remember that day? How many times had his screams and cursing awakened him in the night? How many times did that boy's blank eyes peer at him in his dreams? How many times had he cursed God for the deaths in his congregation?

Whispering under his breath through clenched teeth while looking purposefully toward the sky through the one window, he growled, "You're to blame for this. I trusted You, and You failed me. I'll never trust You again."

The boiling liquid hitting the fire startled him. He cursed his ruined meal.

Since the day the preacher had arrived at this abandoned chickee, no one had ever visited him. He preferred it that way. He demanded it that way. It was part of his punishment for failing his congregation. But today, his self-imposed exile was disturbed by a lone dugout poling silently toward the hut. A tall, dark-skinned Seminole dressed in a native hand-made long shirt of green calico stood naturally balanced in the stern gazing at him from a distance. His appearance mirrored the costume of those long dead from the Seminole Wars. His head wrapped in a traditional turban with Ostridge feathers sticking up in the back. His waist wrapped with a belt of cloth tied in a knot with long tails hanging almost to his knees. He was barefoot.

When the dugout was within shouting distance, the preacher hollered out the front door, "What the hell do you want? I thought you folks didn't come this far in. Superstitious crap or somethin.'" His hand unconsciously clenched the wooden spoon tightly as if it were a formidable weapon.

Without responding, the Seminole remained unmoving in the dugout's stern. He looked intently at the preacher. The preacher felt a sense of almost defensive fear as the Seminole stared at him through his dark eyes. He did not smile as the bow of the dugout came to a rest against the dock. Standing perfectly still, the Seminole balanced both feet on either side of the hand-carved wooden canoe; the preacher noticed the long machete stuck unsheathed in the Seminole's cloth belt. He wondered if the Indian had come to reclaim this chickee.

Rising from his pot, the preacher stepped outside and faced this intrusion arriving at his self-imposed hell.

"Listen, if you're thinkin' that this here hut belongs to you, I came upon it by accident and found it abandoned. I figur' it's mine now. So, I suggest you just mosey on outta here and leave me be."

Now silence in a swamp is not real silence. It is always noisy with the sounds of its creatures and shifting waters against the mangrove shoreline. It's something that after a while one just gets accustomed to, but at this moment the preacher became aware of just how loud it all sounded. Maybe it was his conscience. Maybe it was his guilt. Maybe the Seminole disturbed the swamp's silence. The preacher knew there was something about this man that certainly disturbed him.

Suddenly the silence changed as the Seminole spoke.

"I heard you cry out, and I smelled your pain in the burnt meal."

The preacher had heard that the Seminole had almost spiritual insight into the minds of men. Could his pain have brought the Indian here? Or was it his anger? Or perhaps it was his shame for failing his congregation. He glanced toward the sky and whispered a curse to the One he blamed for probably sending the Indian to torment him further.

Suddenly the preacher's shoulders slumped, and his defensive posture disappeared. He almost dropped the wooden spoon he still held in his hand absently. He then did what he never thought he would do; he invited the Seminole to share his meager meal. The preacher needed to know what brought this Indian so deep into the swamp, and he wanted to keep an eye on that machete.

"Well, come on in. It ain't much, but you can partake. That is if you don't mind burnt cabbage."

The Seminole gracefully stepped from the dugout without so much as a ripple disturbing the water. Silently he followed the preacher into the chickee.

Both men sat squatting on the floor in front of the fire. The preacher stirred the pot one more time, angered that it was now being divided with someone who was not wanted. He had no one to blame but himself. He was the one who invited the stranger.

"I ain't got but one spoon, so we have to share."

Silently the two men passed the spoon back and forth until the pot was empty. Strangely, the preacher's belly felt satisfied. He had never felt such contentment from his pot before. He swore that some of the cabbage tasted just like fish.

Standing and taking the pot to rinse at the water's edge and then filling it as he returned to the fire, the preacher said without looking at the Seminole, "I'll build us some coffee."

From his meager supplies, he threw in a small handful of coffee grounds, some ground corn, and some chicory. They both sat in silence as they watched the pot for a boil.

"Gotta share a cup, too," the preacher said as he handed it to the Indian. He surprised himself with his courteous action. It came from somewhere in his past. It belonged to him before the anger.

"Why do you believe it was your god who killed your people? You believe in *a truth*, but is it *the truth*?" the Seminole spoke without looking up. He then slowly turned his face to the preacher and demanded with his eyes the preacher search his heart before answering.

Truth? The preacher wasn't sure what truth was lately. Truth to him was as he made it. He never considered that truth could exist outside of his own heart and mind. To do so would mean that all he had accumulated in his mind over the years had to be tossed out, and he would have to begin again assembling truth.

Could he risk that?

Would he dare?

This frightened the preacher. How dare this Indian challenge his truth. But perhaps it was because this Indian maybe knew more about truth than the preacher ever pretended to know. It was the one thing he had admired over the years about these people. They seemed to know beyond the white man's knowing.

The preacher stared back as the horror of his truth began from somewhere deep inside. He stood and walked over to the open door and looked out into the swamp, searching for some way to escape this moment. The loud silence of the swamp appeared to roar back at him. The fear he felt came from the idea that his truth once told might reveal a flaw. Then he slowly began.

"They call me Cottonmouth Mather. My people come from a direct line to a founder of this country, Cotton Mather. I never did set out to be no preacher. It began when I was but a boy. There was a cottonmouth what bit me while choppin' wood one day, but the poison didn't take. Everyone figur'd I was charmed by God 'cause of my people, and they started askin' me to give revelation over their ailments and such. It just kinda grew from there. People took to my speakin' and started gatherin' regularly. Next thing I knew, I was their preacher. At first, things happen'd. Folks got healed. Folks got set free from their torments and started turnin' from their evil ways. There was drunks that just stopped drinkin'. Men stopped beatin' on their women. Landlords stopped throwin' folks off their land just 'cause the crops didn't make enough for the rent. Folks just all the sudden started gettin' along. Why we even took to breakin' bread kinda regular like. There was even money in the collection basket now and then.

"I started believin' I was indeed charmed. But the responsibility got to be too much. I got more and more dangerous with my truth of God's ways. It was like goin' to a circus sideshow—I even had the tent. Then one day, this here feller named of George Went Hensley showed up, and he started a-talkin' about handlin' deadly serpents as a sign of true righteousness. He claimed that if'n you was to pick up a rattler and even if'n it bit you, and you did not suffer, then you was a true child of God. He said I was already proof of that.

"So, I swallowed my fear and started holding up serpents in the meetin'. Eventually, I got so used to it that no fear ever came to me. I convinced folks that it was the devil what made them afraid. They believed me, and they began to hold high the serpents. Folks was comin' for miles around to be part of what we's doin'. And then it happened!"

The preacher's shoulders slumped again as he turned slowly back to the Seminole with tears in his eyes; he looked to the floor and whispered, "That was the day God turned on me. That's my truth as I see it."

He then looked up, and the anger had returned to his heart as he expected the Indian to agree with him that God was responsible. Instead, the Indian sat squatting on the floor, seeming to contemplate the preacher's words while turning the cup of coffee back and forth in his hands.

After what seemed like too long, he looked out the open door and quietly spoke, "Someone's coming."

At first, the preacher didn't see anyone on the water. Then he thought he could make out the shape of another dugout poling quickly toward the chickee hugging the mangrove shoreline. A woman was hollering something the preacher did not understand at first. As she got closer, he could just make out her words. She was yelling for him.

"Preacher! Preacher, my boy! My boy is dying! Help me, preacher!"

Stepping out to the dock as she ran the dugout aground, he could hear the terror in her voice. He saw the panic in her eyes. The Seminole slipped up beside him in silence.

"Preacher! My boy got bit by a swamp lion! Help me, preacher! They say in the village you got the gift to save him. Don't let my boy die. He's all I got! Ask your God to save him."

Looking down into the dugout, the preacher saw a young boy lying in the bottom wrapped in a blanket. He had seen those eyes of dying before. Then looking back at the woman he said without emotion as he turned away, "There's nothin' I can do. Nuthin' God will do. Must be He's mad at you for somethin'. Take your boy away and bury him. I cain't help no more."

"Please! Pleeease! You got to do something. He's just a boy. Surely your God will have mercy on him. He ain't lived enough to do no wrong. Please help him!"

Turning back to face her, the preacher yelled with all the anger he had toward God, "I DON'T HAVE NO GIFT! I couldn't save my own people! What makes you think I can save yours? There's nothin' I can do for your boy no more. Nothin'! Not sure I ever could. Please! Just leave me alone. Leave me and go bury your boy."

Jumping down from the dock into the mud next to the canoes, the Seminole searched through the swamp weeds and pulled some which he quickly put into his mouth and began to chew. He placed the poultice on the boy's wound and, removing his belt, he wrapped it tightly and then covered the boy up with the blanket.

"Change the poultice every morning and night. He will recover."

The woman's anguish turned to hope as she knelt and covered the feet of the Seminole with kisses. Someone had given her hope, and she took it as truth. This was her truth. She believed it was the truth.

The Seminole, humbled and seemingly embarrassed by the woman's open display of adoration, encouraged her back into the dugout and eased it into the water, watching as she wept with joy and poled away until she was no longer in sight. He rejoined the preacher on the dock without saying a word.

"Why did you do that? You saw that kid. He was good as dead already! Why did you give her false hope?"

Looking the preacher in the face and searching his eyes, the Seminole said quietly, "Why do you say it was your God that harmed the boy? Don't you teach that your God is a God of love? Why don't you blame the one who brings pain? Why don't you blame the Serpent?"

The Indian's words shocked the preacher as if he had back-slapped him. His anger burst out upon the Seminole. That anger was as much for the One above as it was for the one standing there.

"Damn you! How dare you challenge my truth! You have no idea what it's cost me!"

Raising his fist as if to strike, he yelled, "Blame the Serpent! Blame the Serpent? How dare . . . how dare you tell me who's responsible! Me! Just because you chewed up a few herbs and spit on a snakebite while passing out false hope doesn't make you no healer. I'm the healer! I'm the one people come to! I'm the one God chose! I'm the One!"

The preacher's anger even silenced the swamp, and the silence echoed his words over and over until he heard them.

Quietly, the Seminole said, "If you think you alone have all the answers, then the truth will come harder, and with it, there will be greater pain."

Watching the preacher's eyes for any chance of understanding, he saw nothing. So, turning quickly and without a sound, he jumped down from the dock to his dugout and picking up his long pole pushed out into the water and was gone.

The Seminole's appearance unsettled the preacher for days. Even though the Indian had said little, his words had a way of creeping into the swamp's noisy silence at night. The only good, if you can call it good, was the preacher's dreams were no longer of the dying boy's eyes lying on a dirty concrete floor. In fact, there were no dreams at all—only the silence of the swamp. And the silence had never been so loud. The preacher blamed God for the silence.

Several days later, he decided it was time to make his way to a trading post to replenish his meager supplies. Paddling with the tide, he made quick progress downriver. An eagle caught his eye as he felt the sun shining down on him. For just a moment, the preacher felt this wilderness, and he belonged. Adjusting the canoe with his paddle to avoid a snag barely visible, he realized too late the snag was moving. It rose up as he passed over and the canoe tipped, spilling him into the dark water. He felt a powerful grip on his leg as the ancient reptile dragged him down. In an instant, he knew that the gator would hold him under and roll until he could no longer resist. His lungs panicked for air, and he screamed through the black water for mercy.

And mercy came.

Suddenly the monster released him, and he pushed up to the surface. Grabbing the side of his canoe, he flung himself back in and laid on his face while the terror forced the water from his lungs. Turning over with his face to the sun, he saw the wounds and blood that was filling the bottom of the canoe. Squinting in the sunlight, he heard the eagle's cry overhead. Again, he knew mercy had come.

It seemed hours that he lay there while the tide carried him along. It was then he became aware that his anger had stayed under the water as well as his cursing. The eagle flew high over him, keeping a watchful eye, and he slept.

His nightmares had drowned as well.

The canoe came to rest just above the docks to the trading post. Several men helped him to the store where they bandaged his leg. Many remarked he was lucky. He knew it was something greater than luck.

Again, he slept.

When he awoke, he noticed the pain in his leg had subsided. Rising on his elbows, he looked around the small room at the back of the trading post. His eyes settled on what appeared to be an old, large painting of a Seminole Indian with a traditional headdress and feathers sticking up, a green calico long-shirt, and a cloth belt. The Seminole's eyes were familiar.

14

Shoppin' in Your BVD's

I got this buddy of mine named Jimmy. Jimmy is what you would call—how should I say this—a bit weird. Now, it was the late Sixties, but Jimmy went way past Sixties' weird. I mean he was teachin' his four-year-old son to piss on the highway while hikin' his leg like a dog and waving at the traffic kinda weird. Jimmy was married to a beautiful lady by the name of Kristine. She knew about Jimmy's weirdness. In fact, she often joined him in his strange and unpredictable behavior.

I remember Richard's first wedding when Jimmy and I were part of the wedding party. Jimmy came over to me during the reception and told me with a worried look on his face that some girl was flirting with him, and Kristine saw this woman rubbing herself and gyrating in place in an attempt to get his attention. He was really concerned that Kristine was going to go ballistic on him. I asked him to point out the flirtatious woman, and he discreetly pointed across the room to a blonde whose actions with her eyes, hands, and mouth definitely suggested she was trying to entice Jimmy. Jimmy began to tighten his grip on my arm as he whispered in a panicked voice, "She's comin' this way! Whata I do? Kristine is gonna freak out!"

The blonde woman made her way over to Jimmy and started rubbing herself all over him as he continued his panic. Then it happened! Kristine saw what was going on from across the room and started angrily toward Jimmy.

"Oh, shit! Oh, shit! Kristine is coming!" he muttered as he attempted to pull away from the blonde and hide behind me. "Do something! Tell Kristine this chick thinks I am someone else. Anything! Just don't let Kristine think that I am enjoyin' this."

Then what I never in my wildest fantasies imagined would happen, happened. Kristine walked up to the blonde and started rubbing and kissing her. I freaked! What the hell!

Jimmy's tone changed to serious when he said, "MJ, I'd like to introduce you to my younger sister, Mary."

Mary smiled the same mischievous smile that her brother would smile after pulling a prank on someone successfully. And then after he was satisfied that he had freaked me out, he would add his signature line, "Folks is too frigid nowadays."

Yeah, that was Jimmy.

Jimmy and Kristine lived for a while in a VW camper bus. They would move it around from campground to campground and sometimes even park it on the beach at Jupiter. Richard and I went for a visit during Christmas one year while the bus was parked at a community park in Lake Worth. Kristine had started a coconut palm in a pot that they carried around from place to place. Like I said, it was Christmas, so she hung a lone red ornament from the tree. Nothing better than Christmas in south Florida with sandals, cut-offs, and a decorated palm tree. When we arrived, Kristine and Jimmy had their bath towels and were headed to the public showers.

Jimmy exclaimed with a mischievous grin, "Kristine gave me shower soap paints as an early Christmas present, so we're using 'em tonight. You guys have a sit and roll one. We'll be back in a little bit."

Kristine giggled as she ran ahead of Jimmy to the cinder-block building located in the middle of the campground. The overhead light that usually illuminated the front entrance was out. Kristine and Jimmy went in on the women's side of the showers.

Richard threw me a baggie with some Zig-Zag papers, and I sat cross-legged on the ground with a black, 175-gram Frisbee in my lap to roll on. Wherever I went that black Frisbee went with me. You never knew when someone needed a throw, or you might need a rolling tray. As I was licking the paper, I heard a woman scream from the darkened showers. Peering over my round, yellow-tinted glasses, I smiled naughtily at Richard as we both concluded with our laughs that some lady had walked in on Kristine and Jimmy covered in soap paint.

That's Jimmy. Anything to shock, and I'm sure he told the frightened lady that society is way too frigid nowadays.

Like I said, it was the late Sixties. Everything we did was usually coming from the idea that the socially-accepted norms were no longer apropos. We wanted to challenge, we wanted to test, we wanted to shock, we wanted to disrupt. Nothing was off-limits. Nothing and nobody. From little ol' blue-haired ladies to suit-and-tie patrons at the local church.

Enter the Jesus Freaks.

My first public display of the counterculture's design to challenge the status quo happened when an overzealous youth minister who had a religious conversion at Woodstock decided to educate the local young kids on the evils of rock and roll. To illustrate the devil in the music, he used Pink Floyd's album, *Ummagumma*. After playing some random samples, which I deemed too short an offering for convincing proof, he asked if there were any questions convinced he had thoroughly chased away any desire for this sin. My hand went up immediately, and my mother who was in the back of the room lowered her head shamefully knowing what I was going to ask.

"Where can I get that album?"

That was the beginning of the end for my descent into the so-called bowels of hell. It was my first split from the Church and my mother's hope for my redemption. It was the opening of my consciousness into the truths proclaimed loudly by Marshall amps and Fender guitars. I would now worship at the altar of the gods of rock and roll. The path before me was clearly marked and trodden by long-haired hippies. They were the new prophets. They proclaimed loud and clear that there was a new communion to be observed. They would lace the communion wafers with acid.

Ah, acid!

Ahh, the revelation!

Ahhh—the colors!

And Jimmy was one of the new prophets.

Jimmy introduced me to acid in the restroom of the Polo Grounds Fried Chicken restaurant there in West Palm Beach. I had started working there during the summer with Jimmy, and we would often take our breaks to smoke some weed in the Men's bathroom whose entrance was located outside of the restaurant in the alley. Jimmy had been talking about this new hallucinogenic drug known as Orange Sunshine. About the size of a Saccharine tab, Jimmy said it was best if we quartered it. He was not sure we could still function behind the grill while *trippin'* on acid.

Jimmy was right. I don't remember how many chicken wings managed to fly out of the hot grease and out an open window to their freedom before I peaked and started to come down.

After our shift, Jimmy and I drove to Singer Island to score some more acid. Singer Island had become the K-Mart of dope. All one had to do was walk down the center of the parking lot, and individual pushers would holler out their items along with their prices. The police didn't seem interested in busting anyone there. They waited until you drove away and then pulled you over. The trick was to slip out while they were busy with someone else.

After scoring, Jimmy and I headed up to Blowin' Rock in Jupiter. We had heard there was a party there, so naturally, we followed the smoke. When we got there, we didn't see any cars but one. I thought I recognized it as Paul's car, so I ran over and started to beat on the doors and hood so as to annoy Paul and his date.

But it wasn't Paul.

Someone I had never seen before got out along with this half-dressed chick and started yelling at us to get the hell out of there or he was going to shoot us in the ass, or something like that. We didn't wait around for clarification.

We ran down to the beach, laughing at the mistake, when I noticed the sand around our feet was exploding. Now usually this spray of sand is caused by fiddler crabs, but I remarked that the fiddlers seemed mighty big this time of the year. The waves crashing on the reef made it difficult to hear, so Jimmy and I had to shout. He cupped his hands together and yelled into my ear that he didn't think it was fiddlers when another blast of sand blew up in front of us. Jimmy turned and shouted at me to run like hell as he began to zig-zag down the beach, yelling the whole time that folks are too frigid nowadays. It turns out the guy in the car was still mad, and he was unloading a pistol at us.

Well, all of that excitement got us to thinking about heading to Miller's Grocery to satisfy a bad case of the munchies. I worked the night shift at Miller's, and it was famous for its in-house donuts. I would help the night manager make these most excellent creations and often would bring my evening's pay home in fried dough and powdered sugar and cinnamon.

When we pulled into the parking lot, I noticed Jimmy had been awfully quiet since we left Blowin' Rock. I figured he was still freakin' out about being shot at, but Jimmy's not one to freak easily. He is usually the one doin' the freakin'. Finding a parking spot near the front, I shut off the Bug and turned to look at Jimmy. Then I knew.

Now let me say something here about my friend, Jimmy. Whenever Jimmy is quiet, he's thinkin'. He's thinkin' about how to mess with folks who he said were always too frigid nowadays. Yeah, Jimmy's brush with death definitely had him scheming on how to shake up folks. He told me later that the guy shootin' at us was a prime example of a society that needed to do their love makin' on the hood of the car and not hiding in the back seat. We're all too frigid he would declare, and then he would do something that most people, in their wildest fantasies, would never do.

"Ever wonder how people would react if you went shoppin' in your underwear?" he said, staring off into somewhere beyond Miller's.

Now know this about Jimmy, when he says, 'ever wonder' about anything, he's about to test that wonderin' out.

And sure enough, he got out of the car and out of his clothes. Fortunately for the folks shopping inside, Jimmy had on some white BVDs. Usually, we didn't wear anything under our jeans—remember it was the Sixties.

Jimmy grabbed a shopping cart and headed in through the front doors. I started the car.

After what seemed like twenty minutes or more, Jimmy came out with several bags of groceries. I'm still not sure where he had put his money. No one was chasing him, so he calmly put the groceries in the back seat and then got dressed. As soon as he got seated in the car, I took off, half expecting the fuzz to come tearin' into the lot with lights flashin' and sirens blarin'. We made our getaway without incident.

Stopping at the intersection for a red light, I looked over at Jimmy who was starin' again into that place that often only he sees. I had to know.

"Well? What did they do?"

Without looking at me, he replied, "Nothin'. I pushed the cart up and down every aisle, and the only thing they did was move away from me when they saw me comin'. The manager never even came down from his high perch to yell at me. It was rather disappointin'."

Pausing for a moment, he added, "Guess folks ain't as frigid as they used to be."

15

The Case of Barn Burnt

Ever wonder how many ice cubes it takes in a whiskey glass to make it cold enough that the other cubes don't melt? Funny what one thinks about while sitting on a barstool waiting for a dame. Meanwhile, a pal slid into the stool next to me, Professor Winston Harvey Jones. He ordered a whiskey, no ice.

Without looking up, I said, "What brings you to this fine hash-house, Jones?"

"Farley, why is it that from time to time you morph into some 1940s private dick? You got to stop reading all those Chandler and Hammett tales. You worry me sometimes, Farley."

"Occupational hazard, I guess. Comes from too many years teachin' Lit and practicin' sluethin' on the side."

"Say, I didn't take you for the kinda guy that buys his booze at a place like this."

"I come here for the music."

"Really! Didn't take you for a jazz lover either."

"I'm a real mystery, Jones. But, if you must know, I'm meetin' someone here, so if you don't mind just scram before she gets here."

After slugging down his drink and ordering another, Jones turned and with furrowed brow said, "Oh no, I'm not leaving this stool until I see what the great Professor Woody Farley has on the line."

At that moment the door opened and in walked Miss Audrey Feinbody, the departmental secretary. We had arranged to meet here on the edge of town to lessen the scuttlebutt that would certainly happen once the university found that we had stepped out. Leaning close to Jones' ear, I whispered that Feinbody and I were meeting to discuss a case I was looking into and since we all gotta eat . . . well, you know. I then gave Jones a wink. Jones nodded subtly and then winked back as Feinbody walked up.

Smiling and extending her hand, Feinbody said, "Professor Jones, so nice to see you. Will you be joining us for dinner?"

"Please call me Harv. Now if Farley here had asked me that, I'd probably declined, but since the invite comes from such a lovely lady as yourself, I believe I will join you. What'd ya say, Farley, three a crowd?"

As we moved to a table, Feinbody whispered in my ear, "Sorry, I didn't think he would actually accept. I was just being nice."

"Don't worry, I'll get rid of him, but for now Jones might be able to help. He's something of an authority on Faulkner. Let's see if he can shed any light on what's in this package."

Handing the package to Jones, I said, "Take a look at this manuscript I received two days ago. It appears to be an early draft of Faulkner's 'Barn Burning.' It came with this letter from someone claiming to be a relative of Sarty Snopes. He says that Abner Snopes was falsely accused of burning Major de Spain's barn. The letter said this copy was found in a secret place in the apartment where Faulkner lived while staying in New Orleans, and it suggests that Faulkner was not convinced Abner did what was later claimed by de Spain. It goes on to say that Faulkner wrote the story based on a true account."

"What do you think, Dr. Jones?" Feinbody asked in a low whisper while looking around the room for anyone listening in on their conversation.

"First off, 'Barn Burning' is a work of fiction," Jones said amused with the prospect that someone believed the story to be real. "There never has been any indication that he wrote from a real event. That's just preposterous."

"Not according to this letter," I said, handing it to him. "Just think of the possibility. What if this letter is genuine?"

Jones' began to peruse the letter's contents, and his immediate fascination revealed he was no longer interested in having dinner with Feinbody and me for the sake of gossip. While he stood stuffing the manuscript and the letter back into the package, he asked without turning around if he could borrow it and excused himself as he headed for the door. Without looking back, he said he would see us both later. Then, he was gone.

Feinbody smiled across the table at me, and I went all limp. Not something common for Woody Farley with any doll.

It looks like it might be a night of gossip after all.

The next morning, before I could get my office door unlocked, Jones came running up the hall waving the manuscript.

"Farley, we need to go to New Orleans."

"What?"

Pointing to a place in the margin, Jones said excitedly, "See here where Faulkner writes that he wasn't convinced Abner was guilty of what de Spain accused him of just like you said last night. But the actual pages that lay that part of the plot out are missing from this copy that you have. Now Faulkner worked on this draft when he was living in New Orleans in '25. And look here," Jones pointed with his finger to the page, "Faulkner wrote that he kept a copy of this manuscript in a wall behind a bookshelf. I bet those pages could still be there; that is, providing the one who wrote the letter is trustworthy, and this story is based on fact.

"So, whaddya say Farley? Does Sherlock need a Watson?"

A few days later, Jones and I found ourselves standing outside of 624 Pirates Alley. Faulkner lived here while working on *Soldiers Pay*. He had come here as a friend of Sherwood Anderson, and, from what I learned, they were a couple of characters. To our left was the Pirates Alley Cafe, and directly behind us was the St. Louis Cathedral. I decided we needed a drink, so we settled into a corner table of the café, which had two open walls to the intersecting alleys, and ordered.

The rain began to fall lightly.

Jones asked, "So, what's the plan? How are we going to get in and find those missing pages?"

"Not sure yet. We don't even know if the pages are there."

"Well, we at least need to get in and check it out. Who knows, we might get lucky, Farley."

"Farley? Woody Farley, is it really you?" The voice came from a priest standing in the alley with rain dripping from his black umbrella. It sounded familiar, but at that moment I couldn't place it.

"Farley, it's me, Kurt, Kurt Billings from West Palm. My gosh! We graduated from high school together. Between us, we snorkeled the whole south coast of Florida. Why, we even dated the same girls—not at the same time of course," he said with a smile, winking as he nodded to Jones.

Now I remembered. Kurt and I ran around together until I went off to college, and he went off to war.

"Kurt! What the hell are you doing here, and when did you become a priest? I didn't think they'd let someone like you *in* the church, much less to become one of their sky pilots."

Grabbing a chair, Father Kurt shook out his umbrella and leaned it against a column. As he sat down, he motioned with three fingers to the waitress.

"Ah, it happened after the war. You know what they say—soldiers find faith in a foxhole. Well, it's true, or at least in my case, it is. After seminary they gave me my first parish," and pointing his thumb over his shoulder at St. Louis, he continued, "and twenty years later here I am sittin' in a bar with my old pal, Woody Farley. So, what brings you to New Orleans?"

After introducing Jones and revealing that indeed I had grown up in South Florida, a detail that Jones says he was unaware of, I told Father Kurt about going off to college and then becoming a professor while moonlighting as a part-time shamus. I also confided in him about Faulkner's missing pages. Figured we could use someone who knew their way around this town, and, besides, he was a priest. If you can't trust a Bible-thumper with a collar, who can you trust?

"Well, I don't know anything about these missing pages, but I can tell you to watch your step when it comes to the de Spains. They own practically everything around here, including Faulkner's old apartment. They're prominent members of my parish, and they're used to getting their way. You be careful around Armand de Spain; he's the patriarch and mean as a snake. I wouldn't put it past him to have the missing pages."

Swallowing the last of his drink, Father Kurt rose and shook Jones' hand, then he turned to me, "Farley, it's good to see you after all these years. Drop by the church before you leave town. We have a lot to catch up on. Like I said, watch your step!"

As he moved toward the alley raising his umbrella, he turned and asked seriously, "Say, Farley, do you know what happened to Betsy?"

Picking up my glass and slowly pouring the contents down my throat, I thought about what to say. Then without looking at the priest, I said quietly, "No, I lost track of her after high school. Heard she might have married some big shot up north."

Father Kurt could tell he better leave this alone for now and waved as he wandered back across the alley to the church. The rain fell harder.

"Well, it looks like this story *is* based on fact. The good Father there confirms the existence of the de Spain family."

Then with a smirk on his face, Jones asked, "So, Farley, who's this Betsy?"

"Leave it be, Jones. Subject's closed."

"Ok," Jones replied, burying the thought for another time and said, "Hey, I need to hit the head."

I didn't have the courage to tell Father Kurt or Jones that Betsy was the one case I had not been able to solve. Maybe someday.

Easing back into his chair and ordering another round, Jones sat there smiling like he'd just hit the jackpot or something.

"What's got you all smiles?" I asked.

Leaning close so he wouldn't be overheard, Jones said, "I found a way into Faulkner's apartment. There's a window over the john, and it opens up to another that drops into Faulkner's place. I could squeeze through and hide out there until it's safe to let you in. What'd ya think, Farley?"

Jones was determined to play out his role in this whole affair. It was a dangerous move, but right now, it was the one move that might get us into the apartment without notice. I had to agree with Jones; it was a good plan. He smiled even bigger and then downed his whiskey as we discussed the particulars. The rain would help cover any noise we might make.

Around closing time, Jones went again to the bathroom while I paid our tab. I left alone and waited down the alley for the barmaid to close. Then I quietly tapped on the door to the apartment, and, after a few moments, Jones opened it and let me inside. Working quickly, and mostly in the dark so that we wouldn't draw any attention from outside, I soon realized that even though Jones was a willing participant, he lacked the discretion one needs to case a joint in the dark. It didn't take long before he stumbled over something and made enough noise to bring any flatfoot making his rounds. When we felt sure no one was coming to investigate, we continued to search. Locating a bookcase at the back of the apartment, I began to tap quietly between the shelves listening for any hollow spots. The bookcase went all the way to the ceiling, so I called Jones over to boost me up on his shoulders.

Tapping around near the ceiling, I finally found a hollow spot and pried loose some boards, but the hole was empty. A noise from behind caused Jones to turn with me still suspended on his shoulders, and I came spilling down. Standing in the doorway was a man pointing a bean-shooter and a flashlight at the both of us.

"Just what the hell are you two doing in my apartment and what the hell are you looking for?"

Carefully picking myself up off the floor, I figured this was Armand de Spain. He didn't look too happy standing there, dripping in the rain. Jones wasn't too tickled either with having a piece pointed at him as we both raised our hands.

"I asked what the hell you two are doing in my apartment! You know I got every right to shoot you both for breaking and entering. So, what's it going to be, you going to give me some answers, or do I start puttin' holes in you?"

Now, like I said, Jones is a novice when it comes to B and E, so he nervously begins telling some story about being drunk and stumbling into the wrong building. It didn't sound too convincing, but we had been drinking, so I played along.

"He's telling the truth, mister," I said, indicating Jones. "We were next door, and they threw us out when we reached our limit. We just kinda stumbled against the door and it swung open. We thought it was our hotel room. Honest mister, we don't mean no harm . . . . You mind lowerin' that piece a bit."

"They're telling the truth, de Spain," came that familiar voice from the alley. "I saw them leave the bar and just like they said, they fell against the door and it popped open. You must not have locked it securely last time you were here."

Surprised by the priest standing behind him in the alley in the rain, de Spain said with disgust, "Well, if Father Kurt here vouches for you, I guess I believe him. But don't let me catch either of you around here again—got it!"

De Spain made sure the door was secure as we left with Father Kurt, and I muttered a thank you as we headed back down the alley with rain dripping off of my Fedora. Jones shared Kurt's umbrella. When we were safely out of earshot of de Spain, I turned and asked Father Kurt just what sort of providence brought him out this late at night.

"I couldn't sleep, so I was on my way to prayers. I saw de Spain at the door with his gun and knew that wasn't good. I told you to steer clear of him. He's trouble."

Jones finally recovered his nerve and thanked Father Kurt for intervening. He also promised to come to services for a year to do penance for almost getting us shot. Father Kurt told him it wouldn't be necessary, but that running with me probably would lengthen his time in Purgatory.

"Thanks for the confidence, Kurt, but I don't get a rod shoved in my face every time."

"Did you find what you were looking for?" the priest asked.

"No, I found the hiding place Faulkner used, but I saw it was empty just before Jones here dropped me. My guess is either Faulkner destroyed the pages, or de Spain possibly found them. Think I'll pay him a visit to find out later, but now I got to get some shut-eye. Thanks again for steppin' in. Say, are you gonna get in trouble with 'you know who' for lying?" I said, pointing my finger upwards.

"I think stopping de Spain from shooting you outweighs the stretching of the truth. Goodnight, Farley, and Jones, be careful around this guy—he's trouble," said Father Kurt smiling as he wandered off in the direction of the church.

The rain began to recede.

The next morning, I looked up de Spain's address so Jones and I could pay him a visit. Confronting him face to face might reveal to me if he indeed had the missing pages. It probably wasn't my best plan, but I didn't have a lot of time, and I also didn't have any new leads.

A knock at his door brought a beautiful doll with long blonde locks and gorgeous gams. This dame caught me off guard for a moment, but I quickly recovered and asked if de Spain was in. She smiled slightly and looked us both up and down as she said her father was in and to follow her.

We found de Spain in his solarium, and he was surprised to see us. He asked his daughter, Stella, if she wouldn't mind leaving us alone for a bit, and, as she turned to leave, she gave me a wink and walked away slowly. She didn't need eyes in the back of her head to know I was watching. She was confident that every man watched her walk away.

Quickly changing his tone to anger, de Spain asked, "Now, would you mind telling me what you two are doing here. I assume that last night was not a drunken mistake, and you were looking for something, weren't you?"

"Name's Farley, and this here is Jones. I'm a private dick looking into a case for a client. Name of Snopes. Ring a bell?"

I knew it wasn't a smart move to play my hand this early, but I had to see de Spain's reaction, and I needed to know if he could be rattled. He played it cool, but not before he shifted his eyes and swallowed hard. I could tell I had tightened the screws.

"Snopes! Yeah, I know Snopes. That family's been a boil on my family's butt for generations. Whatever he's telling you, whatever he's got you doing, believe me, he's doing it for vengeance. The Snopes have been mad at my family ever since my great-uncle, Major de Spain, caught Abner Snopes burnin' his barn down. I don't know what you're lookin' for, but you're wasting your time, and I suggest that you two head on back home leaving decent folks alone."

"Snopes claims that there's proof that Abner didn't burn down that barn. He claims, in fact, that it was your great-uncle that burned his own barn and blamed Abner. I have an original account of the event by Faulkner, and it confirms that report."

Jones looked cautiously at me then. It certainly unsettled de Spain. He nervously did a mental check of where he had stashed the missing pages. Knowing he'd have to check for himself, he told us to get out and quickly disappeared. As we made our way to the door, Stella appeared from around the corner. I wondered how much she had heard. It was obvious to me she didn't care much for her father. I decided I could use that.

"Leaving so soon, Detective Farley? I was hoping I could get to know you and Mr. Jones a little better while you're in New Orleans. My father is certainly not the best of hosts, so perhaps I could make up for his lack of manners and show you two the town tonight. Do you like jazz?"

Immediately, Jones perked up and responded, "I bet you know where all the hot spots are. When can we pick you up?"

"How about I meet you at the Little Gem Saloon at, say, nine tonight? And wear your dancing shoes," she said with a smile at Jones.

Stepping between Jones and me, Stella pressed herself against me. Her perfume was intoxicating. She slipped something into my pocket and then whispered, "You do dance, don't you, Detective Farley?"

Smiling, she turned quickly as both Jones and I watched her disappear into the house.

"Can you believe it, Farley. We will see the real side of New Orleans jazz with the prettiest gal in the French Quarter. Say—do you know how to dance?"

As soon as we were out of sight of the house, I checked my pocket to see what Stella had stashed there. It was an address, and she had written what looked like a combination below that.

"Looks like you're dancing tonight without me."

It wasn't any trouble convincing Jones to keep our date with Stella at the Little Gem; I headed over to the cathedral to see Father Kurt. He was surprised and glad at the same time that I actually came to see him. I prattled on about the past for a moment, and then I asked him about the address that Stella had given me. He wasn't too pleased about me going down there at night by myself and offered to go with me. I convinced him this was my doing and he'd just get in the way. And besides, I said as I patted my coat pocket, I was carrying the difference. Father Kurt gave me his blessing, and I caught a taxi to the lower side of town. He was right. This was not the place to be late at night without someone at your back. This was a time I could've used Jones.

When the taxi pulled up to a dark warehouse district, I paid the cabbie and hopped out. It didn't take long to locate de Spain's Export Company. Making sure no one was looking, I expertly picked the lock and stepped inside. Striking a match to get the lay of the land, I moved to the back of the building to a small office. It didn't take long for me to locate a floor safe. As I was about to open it, I heard several voices coming from the front of the warehouse. Slipping into a closet, I kept the door ajar so I could hear what was going down. I also could see enough to make out de Spain as he switched on the desk lamp.

The first voice said with urgency, "I'm telling you de Spain, we got to move this stuff before the heat catches up with us. Besides, the Snopes' are breathing down our necks. If we don't do something about them, they're going to take over the east side. And now I hear they got some private dick snoopin' around tryin' to mess things up. Guy's name is Farley or somethin' like that."

"Yeah, I know about Farley. You leave him to me. And don't worry about the Snopes' either, I've been dealing with that white trash for a long time now. They won't move in on my territory, I promise you. Now go on, get out of here; I got work to do!"

After the first voice left, de Spain turned to the other and said, "Now about this problem that needs to go away. I need you to handle it."

"I gotcha. Who and where? Write it down."

Scribbling something on a notepad, de Spain then said, "Name's Farley. He's stayin' at the Hotel Monteleone."

"Consider it done," and the second voice left.

De Spain then reached down into the floor safe. After removing its contents, he switched off the lamp and left. I knew I had to get to Jones before he got back to the room, but someone else decided to slip into the warehouse. He didn't use a key. He quietly opened a side door and let in others. In the darkness, they moved quickly taking inventory out of the warehouse. I decided before they stumbled on me, I better slip out a back window.

I arrived at the hotel just as Jones was falling off a hansom cab, all while doing a poor Brando imitation to the blonde still sitting there, "Stella! Stella!" At that same time, he saw me step out of the shadows and with a great flourish, he yelled, "Farley, my ol' pal and colleague! Come join us for a drink! STELLAAA," he shouted with a wave of his arms morphing back into Brando. "Stella and I have had the most mar-vel-lous time. And you missed it!" he said, punctuating his words by stabbing me in the chest with his finger several times. Then Jones tripped over his own feet right into the doorman who was attempting to quiet the situation.

"To my room, Max! And, shssish," he said, waving his fingers across his lips, "there's a fiver in it if you get me there before I embarrass myself in front of this lovely lady."

Then looking at me with a wink, Jones remarked, "A fiver! A fiver! Did you hear that, Farley? I said a fiver. Sounded just like you when you're in your private dick voice."

Turning red with embarrassment, Jones looked at Stella and apologized for using profanity in her presence.

Stella looked at me, questioning. She didn't get the reference.

I just shrugged my shoulders as Jones passed out cold in the arms of the doorman.

Looking like this happened way too many times before, the doorman raised his chin toward me as if to ask what did I intend for Jones. So, together we lifted Jones back into the cab. I needed to stash Jones somewhere safe until I could deal with the unwanted visitor. I told the cabbie to head for the cathedral then offered to drop off Stella first, but she insisted we see Jones safe into bed.

"Bring him in and put him in the back there," said Father Kurt running his hand through his unkempt hair. We had to wake him up, and I wasn't sure it was his Christian charity or just the memories of me bringing him home in the same condition when we were in high school that produced his smile. He told Stella not to hang around me too much and then shoved us out the door. I paid the cabbie to drop Stella off at her home and told her I had some unfinished business before the night was through. She leaned out of the cab and whispered for me to be careful, then kissed me, and with a smile that suggested she was not through with me settled back in her seat as they drove away.

Funny, at that moment, I thought of Feinbody.

Waiting in the dark of the room, I heard the door open slowly. A dark figure with a heater pointed in front crept in silently. Moving to the bed, the figure aimed and fired two rounds with a silencer. Just then I flipped on the lights, and the assassin spun around disoriented from the brightness. Two shots and he fell back onto the bed. I searched his pockets and found de Spain's stationery with my name and the Hotel Monteleone on it. Leverage. When the house dick got there, I told him what happened, and he said he'd square it with the cops. He also suggested that I make tracks.

The next day, I went to collect Jones. "What'd ya say, feel up to paying de Spain one more visit?"

Gently rubbing his temples, he whispered, "Farley—I must have laid one on last night. Man, what a head. Say I didn't do anything to embarrass Stella did I? And one more question, why am I in a church?"

After getting Jones some java and beignets, we headed over to de Spain's. Stella met us at the door looking fresh and alluring even after a late night on the town. She assured Jones he had been the perfect gentleman all evening, winking at me. Jones grinned sheepishly.

Meanwhile, de Spain slipped quietly into the room, and looking surprised to see me still standing upright, he asked Stella to please leave us alone and ushered us into the library.

I could tell he was nervous. Then using his nervousness to my advantage, I told him I had had a visitor last night that sent his regrets, but not before singing about de Spain and the missing manuscript. Producing the stationary, I told de Spain unless he gave me the missing Faulkner manuscript, we were all gonna take a ride down to the station house.

At first, de Spain laughed, a laugh that said he had no intention of going anywhere with me. So, I pulled my piece to show I meant business.

He changed his tune.

Retrieving the pages from a desk, he handed them over to me. Handing the pages to Jones to make sure they were what we came for, I told de Spain that I'd hold on to the stationery just in case he got any funny ideas about sending round another late-night visitor.

Jones and I left without telling Stella goodbye. Jones felt it was best since he was certain she had taken a shine to him. I decided not to spoil his fantasy and agreed it was probably the right thing to do.

We decided to have one last drink at the Pirates Alley Cafe before heading out of town. Father Kurt joined us. Both Jones and Kurt were anxious to know what the missing pages revealed. Glancing over them quickly, I handed them to Jones. He, too, skimmed the passage.

Disappointed, he laid the pages on the table and took a big swig of his bourbon.

"There's nothing there that indicated Faulkner truly had evidence to the contrary on de Spain. It appears that Abner did burn the barn," said Jones.

Father Kurt said, "I thought that Snopes fellow believed otherwise."

"He wanted to make us think that so we would come to New Orleans and poke around. The rivalry between the de Spains and the Snopes' goes way back. They are still fighting it out for territory here in New Orleans. Snopes used Jones and me to get de Spain looking elsewhere while they ripped off de Spain's warehouse. I ran into one of Snopes' men last night. They probably had the warehouse empty before I even got back to the hotel."

Raising my glass, I nodded to Jones and Father Kurt, "Gentlemen, here's to another case closed."

We all swallowed our drinks and then together slowly ambled down the alley.

My thoughts turned to the one case I never did solve.

Betsy.

16

The Case of Missing Betsy

"Tell ol' Farley ta give me a ring will ya. It's kinda important," said the voice on the other end of the line.

Miss Feinbody, while trying to restrain her concern, responded with, "I don't know when he will be back in. He hasn't answered any of my calls, and, quite frankly, I'm a bit worried."

"Aw, don't worry 'bout Farley. He's probably held up in some cheap motel workin' some sleazy case, either that or he's on another bender. That Farley, he'll take care of hisself."

"I just wish he'd phone in. He hasn't been back in the office since he returned from New Orleans, but I'll pass on the message as soon as Professor Farley surfaces. Let me get your number, and I will get back with you."

Ever wonder what a cheap motel room looks like from inside a two-week drunk. Believe me, it ain't pretty—especially if you haven't allowed housekeeping in to clean during that time. Who 'da thought that me, Woody Farley, would ever go blind over a dame who hasn't been seen or heard from for over twenty years? Somewhere in this fog of drunk, I suddenly became aware of a banging sound that wouldn't let up. Maybe it was in my head, but something told me that the voice I heard with the banging was more than just drunk fog.

"Farley! Farley, you in there? Open up, buddy. It's Jones and Father Kurt. Come on, Farley, open up—please!" came the voice followed by more banging.

Lowering myself off the bed one limb at a time, I crawled to the door but couldn't seem to navigate the knob. The knob appeared to be way too high for me to reach. Couldn't imagine why the builders would install it where no one could reach it. Finally, it dawned on me that my perception might be slightly off due to the booze and the fact that I was still on my knees, so I came at it again, this time with greater success. After unlocking the door, I found that a new obstacle had presented itself. A body appeared to be blocking the door. Eventually, I deduced that the body was mine. The voice prompted me to move back away from the door, and, again, using one limb at a time, I slowly crawled out of the way.

"Farley, thank God you're alive!" came the words from someone wearing a black Nehru shirt and looking seriously like Father Flanagan. The other guy was tall and had his hair pulled back like Steven Seagal. All of a sudden, I panicked, thinking that they were going to kick my ass and haul me off to Boys Town.

The tall one leaned down with his face close to mine and said, "Farley, it's me, Winston Harvey Jones. We came to take you home, buddy. Think you can stand up?"

Now there was an academic question that, from my perspective, required more research. I postulated that the action could be accomplished by straightening the two appendages located below my waist, but that hadn't been successfully attempted in nearly two weeks. I gave it the old heave-ho, but quickly fell into the arms of the priest. Staring at him, I wondered if someone had died and was that someone me?

"Steady there, Farley," said the priest with some compassion along with a smirk. It was as if he had seen me in this shape before, although I couldn't for the life of me remember when.

Between the two of them they managed to get me into a car, and, after some discussion, they agreed to take me to someone named Feinbody. Feinbody. I was hoping the name matched the person and smiled to myself as I slipped into unconsciousness.

Waking to a beautiful smell, I saw through my bloodshot eyes a figure that made me pray this was Feinbody.

"Well, it's about time you woke up, Professor. You had us all worried to death," came a voice as beautiful as the smell.

I managed the typically confused retort, "Where the hell am I, and who the hell are you, doll-face? Not that I'm complaining, you see, but what are you doin' in this flophouse with me?"

"Professor Farley, you're not in a 'flophouse,' you're in my house," she emphasized with hands on her hips, perturbed by the reference to her home. "You've been asleep for two days now," she responded, and then she appeared to realize I did not know who she was or what had happened the last couple of weeks.

Softening, she said, "Let me get Professor Jones in here, and maybe he can fill you in."

When doll-face and her long, gorgeous gams left the room, I tried to muster the energy to get out of bed then I realized that I didn't have a stitch on . . . . I was curious, where were my rags, and did the dame have anything to do with it and, most importantly, why did I sound like a two-bit private dick in a Bogart film?

"Farley, you old coot! You sure had us worried. What the hell has gotten into you?" asked Jones as he sat on the edge of the bed. Then I guess he realized it was the dame's bed and stood up quickly. He looked at Feinbody, but she didn't seem to notice his embarrassment.

Knocking on the bedroom door, the Father Flanagan character entered apologizing to Feinbody that no one answered the front door, so he let himself in. He turned his attention to me with that earlier smirk and said, "Welcome back to the living, Farley." Quickly realizing the look of confusion on my face, he introduced himself. "It's me, Kurt. Thought I was going to have to give you last rites there for a moment, but I see you're now back."

Me, I wasn't so sure.

It took some doing, but between the three of them, they managed to fill in the pieces of the last two weeks. It seems that, after returning from a case in New Orleans, I disappeared into several bottles of hooch over some doll named Betsy.

There's that Bogart voice again.

I asked Miss Feinbody where my clothes were, and both Father Kurt and Professor Jones looked at one another. Father Kurt had that same smirk I'd seen before. Jones just appeared embarrassed again. Feinbody said she had washed them since I had been rolling around in them for two weeks. She went to get them but didn't offer any explanation as to how she got them off me.

I borrowed Father Kurt's smirk.

Now life after a two-week drunk is something no man should have to endure. Your sensitivities are all off, and the pounding in your head is best left to uninterrupted silence. The line of students waiting outside my door didn't give me much hope that that would be the case today. Miss Feinbody was also waiting with that beautiful smell and a handful of memos of calls that needed answering. One, in particular, she mentioned, sounded urgent. An old flatfoot I knew from back home in Florida by the name of Brunson.

"Farley! Why if you ain't the hardest man ta get a hold of. Where ya been? Workin' a case, eh?"

"Brunson, you still hangin' out at the Opry in Nashville workin' security? Tell me, what can I do for you," I asked, lowering my voice hoping that the voice on the other end would do the same. But with Brunson, it was a forlorn hope. He always was a loud but honest cop who from time to time gave me helpful tips. We hadn't seen each other for years but managed to keep in touch now and then.

"Yeah, still chasin' the strummer's dream. Security work pays the bills; you know how it is. Hey, you remember askin' me a while back ta keep my ear open for any mention of a broad named Betsy Cooper? Well, I got a lead, see, from this pal of mine back home. He says he ran across a Betsy Cooper livin' down south Florida—Delray or Boynton, I think. She matches the profile, so I thought I'd pass it on. You want I should give you the address?"

After hanging up, I noticed my hand was shaking. I didn't know if it was the hangover or the excitement that, for the first time in many years, I finally had a lead on the one case I never could solve.

"You really going all the way to South Florida to look for this Betsy?" Jones asked. "You really shouldn't be taking any more time away from classes after that two-week absence. What do you think the dean will say?"

"I'm not going until the break so that I won't lose any more time. You want to come along?"

"Come along where," asked Feinbody as she entered the office leading a student.

"Where are you two off to this time?" she questioned as she abruptly pointed the confused student to a chair and looked back and forth between Jones and me with her hands on those hips again. Then putting her hands on my desk, she leaned in and demanded, "And just when do you plan on being back, Professor?"

I wasn't sure if it was a genuine concern or maybe frustration at my possible relapse into a bottle again. Either way, as she stood up, leaving that beautiful smell to linger at my desk, I noticed Jones had Father Kurt's smirk.

The student had left. Feinbody had frightened him. She frightened me, but for different reasons I wasn't too sure about. I decided I would figure it out when I got back.

Later that night, there was a knock at the door. Before I could get to it, Father Kurt came wandering into the kitchen. Handing him a bourbon, I inquired as to the reason for the intrusion.

"Jones said you were headed back home to Florida looking for Betsy."

I noticed a grim look on his face that suggested he didn't approve of our travel plans.

"Why the long face? Don't you want to know what happened to her that night after the prom? She was your friend, too, you know."

Swallowing his drink in one gulp, Father Kurt studied my face for the longest time and then he resigned himself to "Good luck, Farley. I'm flying back to New Orleans tonight, so take care of yourself this time. And Farley . . . I hope . . . I hope you finally find what you're looking for."

He left as quickly as he came.

After touching down at Palm Beach International, Jones and I rented a car and drove to the address Brunson had given me. I had the sneaking suspicion that something just wasn't right. A dark depression seemed to hang over me, some nagging memory I couldn't quite recall.

Ringing the doorbell, I heard voices of children inside, and then it came to me at that moment that Cooper was probably a married name. A lady I had never seen before answered the door asking what we wanted. I stared dumbfounded into the face of someone who no matter how I tried, I could not make my lost Betsy. I stammered an apology saying we had the wrong house and sorry we bothered her, and Jones and I headed back to the rental car.

Jones sensing my deep disappointment, asked, "Tell me about Betsy. Why have you been searching for her all these years?"

"It was prom, '64. Me and Betsy Cooper—King and Queen of the prom. Kurt was there also, but he didn't have a date. Not sure why. After the dance, Betsy just kind of disappeared. We searched for hours around the high school and surrounding area and finally decided to drive to her house to see if she was there. That night an idiot ran the stoplight on Main and plowed into the passenger's side of my car. Kurt was hurt pretty bad, and so was I. We both ended up in the hospital for over a month. I never heard from Betsy again. When I got out of the hospital, I left town right away, and I heard Kurt joined the Army. We didn't see each other until that day in New Orleans."

"Man, I'm so sorry this turned out to be a bust," Jones said. "I thought certain you were going to find her. Didn't you check before coming to see if Cooper was a married name? Usually, you're on your game, Farley."

Jones was right. I guess I let my anxiousness in finding out what happened to Betsy cloud my skills as a detective. The old Farley would never have let this happen. Or was it perhaps that darkness that lingered in the back of my mind was putting me off. All I could think about now was getting back to some semblance of normality. I was hoping it would involve Feinbody and that wonderful smell of hers. The case, for now, like before, would remain unsolved.

"I thought you went back to New Orleans," I said, entering my apartment and noticing Father Kurt helping himself to my bourbon. It looked like he had been at it for some time.

"Yeah, well I thought I'd hang around and see how the Florida thing turned out. What did you find?"

"It wasn't her, but then it seems like you already knew that. Say, why are you really here? Don't you have a church to run and souls to save?"

"It's just your soul I'm worried about Farley." Setting his glass down and pushing it away from him, he looked at me with sorrow in his eyes and breathed a deep sigh as he began to speak.

"Farley, it's time for you to remember what happened all those years ago. What happened to you and what happened to me, and what actually happened to Betsy. You've blocked everything from your memory since that night, and it's destroying you. You have got to face your demons! I have, and now it's your turn. I have to make you remember what happened that night."

A cold chill began to run up my spine, like being in a dark alley, and knowing what you're looking for is waiting at the end. I wasn't sure what Father Kurt knew that I didn't, but one thing was certain, the liquor was giving him a reckless determination as he stood and stumbled toward me with anger on his face.

"YOU SON OF A BITCH! YOU'RE THE ONE WHO KILLED HER! YOU NEED TO REMEMBER THAT!" he yelled while clutching me by the collar of my jacket. Through his anger and tears, he lowered his voice and, looking me in the eye, he continued, "You . . . you killed Betsy."

Then he just broke down and fell into my arms weeping. After what seemed like an eternity, Kurt finally composed himself and moved back toward the bottle, but he stopped and turned to face me.

"Farley, you've got to remember what happened that night. We both got really drunk, and I told you that I was in love with Betsy and she was in love with me. You were my best friend, and I stole your girl. You refused to believe it and insisted on driving her home as drunk as you were. I jumped into the back seat to try and reason with you. You ran the stoplight and that car— that car killed Betsy—my Betsy, our Betsy. It was you, Farley. You! And you've blocked that night out of your head since then and somehow have believed this fantasy that Betsy left you that night. You pretend you're some kinda 1940s Philip Marlow trying to solve the case. The one case you couldn't solve. Why did she leave? She did leave you. She left both of us. She's dead, Farley. She's dead, and you're to blame!"

I now know the source of that ever-present darkness. It's the truth of that night. I now know why I couldn't ever solve that case. I've been lying to myself to cover my fault in destroying three lives. But why couldn't I remember? Was it because I didn't want it to be true? Has my whole life from that night been a fabrication of my own reality? I really couldn't remember that night; I didn't want to remember that night.

But, somehow, I knew Kurt had told the truth. It really was all my fault.

I killed Betsy.

17

Puerto Rico French

Ever had one of those *déjà vu* moments when you pass someone or something and it takes you back to a time where you wish you could relive, not just recall? It happened the other day back home in West Palm Beach as I was coming out of Walgreen's drug store. I had gone in to fill a prescription for allergy medicine, and as I was headed to my car, she was getting out of hers. Her side-face profile reminded me of *the One*. You know—*the One*! We all generally have someone in our lives that initiated us into moments of maturity and, for some, forever changed the course of our lives. *The One* taught me how to French kiss in the backseat of a bus in Puerto Rico in 1969. I was 15. Her name was Skyla.

Now I know many of you are saying, "Shit, man! You were 15! What took you so long?" Yes, it's true. Most of my buddies started a few years earlier, or at least that's what they told me. But not me. And it wasn't for lack of trying. Believe me, I tried to learn the mysteries of boy/girl relationships, but I was a fearful and tremulous student.

Let's see. There was the pastor's daughter, Jamie. She chased me and said she wanted to do things her father definitely preached against. I was still sheltered in the *Thou shalt not's*. So I ran.

And then came Pam and Diane. They both wanted to date me at the same time. I'm not talking about going out separately with full knowledge of the other; I mean literally on the same night at the same movie. Two girls at the same time scared the hell out of me. How does one coordinate two girlfriends at once and they know about each other? Yeah, it was great for my reputation, but I wasn't even driving yet. What if one wanted to make-out and the other didn't, or what if they both wanted to make-out at the same time? Who do you kiss first? How long do you kiss one before the other needs kissing? And what if in our *ménage à trois* one of the girls suddenly decides she doesn't like me. Would she have to stay for the whole movie? Should she pay me back for the popcorn and soda? There were too many possible obstacles, and I still lacked experience when it came to kissing and everything else that went along with liking girls. So, I ran.

And, of course, I can't forget Mary. Mary who had developed more than most girls at fifteen. She was every hormone-enraged young boy's fantasy. She certainly was my fantasy, but Mary was looking for someone who knew their way around a bra. So, she ran.

Quite frankly, I had no *hands-on* experience with someone who did not need to stuff their bra with tissue. In fact, my initial experience with tissue boobs was at my first boy-girl dance in the 7th grade. Barbara! When I picked Barbara up, I noticed that Mother Nature had visited her since I last saw her earlier that day. I wasn't sure how it happened so quickly, but I was certainly looking forward to a slow dance. During the dance, we both held on to each other as if we were afraid of someone cutting in. Being so tightly entwined, Barbara's face was only a bare inch from mine, and she decided it was time I kissed her. She pressed her closed lips on mine and held them there for what seemed like hours, but probably was only several minutes. When the music was over, as we parted, her boobs remained crushed. At the time, I thought it was my fault. So, I ran.

Like I said, the opportunities were all around me, but I guess I was afraid that if I tried anything, I'd get my face slapped, and I would lose a girlfriend. Somehow just having a girlfriend was more important than what you could do with one. However, I was beginning to tire of running.

That all changed in the winter of '69. Our South Florida church youth choir had decided to join another from North Carolina and go perform for the churches in the Caribbean. Little did I know I would be the one *born again!*

We landed in Montego Bay, Jamaica, and then took a two-hour train ride up into the mountains of Kendal. The train was crowded because it was the day after Christmas, and the locals were headed home after visiting family on the coast. Now it was not just crowded with people; there were chickens, goats, and a small Christmas pig that wasn't going to see the New Year. Halfway up the mountain, the train broke down for over four hours. It was hot, and there was absolutely no water on the train, so the locals jumped off and ran into the jungle to bring the *white folks* some sugar cane to chew on. It moistened our mouth enough to satisfy our thirst. It was there and then that I first noticed the long, black-haired beauty sitting giggling not more than a few seats in front of me. Every once in a while, she would pretend to look back over the heads of the passengers, but I always managed to lock eyes and get a sly smile from her. I was hoping that, finally, I could stop running.

We flirted with teenage banter while in Jamaica, but by the time we got to Haiti, we were sitting outside the hotel till curfew holding hands. I need to tell you something about our hotel in Haiti. They had an overflow room away from the main building that was made of decorated brick—you know the kind with holes in them big enough to stick an arm through. We decided this was because there was no air conditioning, and the holes allowed the breeze to come inside. On the inside, there was only one solid block wall that separated the bathroom from the bunk beds which lined the outside walls.

Sitting outside on a hotel patio couch on New Year's Eve, Skyla told me about a local who was following her that day in the Iron Market. She was so afraid that when she heard a noise in the bushes in front of us, she jumped closer and her well-developed, 15-year-old body pressed itself hard against me. I could tell she didn't use any tissue. Wanting to make a manly impression, I jumped up and headed for the bushes while assuring her that I would take care of any danger. A dark and thinly muscular man with many scars stepped out of the bushes holding a 14-inch cane knife. He moved toward me, and I froze. Even in the growing darkness, he could see the fear in my eyes. Then as quickly as he appeared, he turned and walked away down the hill into the village where crowds were gathering for the New Year's celebration. Skyla said that was the man, and I suggested we retire for the evening since it was about curfew anyway, and besides, I needed to step behind the solid block wall in the overflow room to check my pants. Holding her body would have to wait until tomorrow when we headed to Puerto Rico.

As I settled in an upper-bunk, I heard the sounds of the villagers coming up the hill toward the hotel. I figured they knew the overflow room was full of young American boys, and I'm sure the guy with the cane knife told them we could be easily spooked. Several held torches that cast an eerie effect on their faces as they surrounded the room and stuck their dark arms through the outside wall's holes and tried to reach us. They laughed and beckoned us with whispered words that we all believed had something to do with voodoo, but no one knew for sure. Those of us still in our beds, at this time, scooted as far away to the edge as we could while shaking with fear. Several boys wet their beds. Me, I had to go back behind the solid block wall again.

The next morning, we packed, and without a word to anyone about what happened, we spent the day sightseeing before heading to the airport. I often wondered what the hotel staff thought of the pile of soaked sheets thrown in the corner of the bathroom.

That evening we landed at Isla Verde Airport a few miles northwest of San Juan. Skyla and I were late getting on the bus because I thought it would be the gentlemanly thing to do to get Skyla's bags too—so, by the time we got on the bus to the youth camp at Juana Diaz, the front seats had already filled up. Fortunately, Skyla and I both had allies who conspired to secure the very back seat on the right side for us. They hailed us back to our own Garden of Eden, which I hoped would yield forbidden fruit. I was planning on disregarding some of the *Thou shalt not's*.

While I held the bags over the heads of the choir members, we scooted down the narrow aisle, and I noticed that our pastor's wife had taken the outside seat just two up from the back and she was sitting sideways with her legs out in the aisle. She pulled them in quickly for Skyla to pass, but just as quickly put them back in the aisle as I tried to navigate the obstacle all the while balancing the luggage. I hit the choir director's son, Ralph, with my Samsonite hard-shell suitcase. He howled and threatened me with language that brought the pastor's wife out of her seat to investigate the ruckus. Using the distraction as an opportunity, I squeezed by her and fell into the back seat next to Skyla. Looking back down the aisle at me, the pastor's wife locked eyes as if she were a holy prophet. I got the sense she was calling down a holy fire upon me, the unholy infidel. I swear I heard a quiet voice, whispering, "Thou shalt not."

After securing our bags under the bus seat, I reached into my shirt pocket for a packet of Beech-nut gum or courtin' wax as my dad called it. Stuffing a piece into my mouth, I offered one to Skyla, but she just shook her head slowly. It was as if she knew what was going to happen and knew gum would only get in the way.

Skyla moved herself up against the window so that as I moved toward her, we were out of the view of anyone in front of us. She wrapped her arms around me and pulled me into her embrace, which placed my face within inches of hers. I could smell her sweet breath and feel its warmth on my face. I knew I was about to engage in some kissing, and I thought my experience up to that moment was complete. Remember, I had kissed Barbara during our slow-dance; however, Skyla was about to teach me what Barbara had left out.

It began with our closed lips pressing hard against each other, but the moment her lips parted, and her tongue entered my mouth, my first instinct was to laugh. I thought she was after my gum. But that idea only lasted a brief second because the next thought was how wonderful. This probing of my own tongue was possibly the most exciting thing I had ever experienced in my 15-year-old life. Even in my deepest religious experiences, I had never felt such ecstasy. I was moving into a higher plane, higher than I had ever been before. Any higher and I would be communing with the angels. I felt certain angels were surrounding me at this very moment and encouraging me to experience the pleasures God had created for man and woman. I opened my eyes just to see if perhaps Skyla was messing with me and trying to gross me out, but it was obviously not what her body language was in any way suggesting.

Surely, she was hearing the angels, too.

My next concern was that the pastor's wife was only a few seats in front of us. Fear came over me, and I was sure that she was going to jump up and pry us apart all the while yelling at us about the *Thou shalt not's* and warning us of the fires of hell and eternal damnation. I imagined she had never heard the angels herself; otherwise, she would be rejoicing in my new-found ecstasy. I closed my eyes and prayed silently to God, the same God that said we can't do these things, and begged Him not to let this end.

I beseech thee oh Lord, do not let that lady stop this! You cannot let her stop this! You must not let her stop this! PRAISE GOD IN HEAVEN—THIS IS THE REAL REASON WE WERE CREATED! Oh, Holy God in Heaven! I do believe in miracles! I do believe in miracles, and surely this is your finest. And I promise if you grant me this one request I will never ask for anything else again. I promise I will be good. I will be good; I will be good, I promise. Just . . . just not right this second. After this girl gets her tongue out of my mouth, then I swear . . . I'll be good! Amen!

Skyla's aggressive probing sent stirrings way down deep into my very soul, and somewhere outside of me, I was hearing the sounds of an angelic choir celebrating along with me and this rapturous moment. I slowly began to realize it was our own choir who had begun to sing Norman Greenbaum's "Spirit in the Sky." Someone was banging a tambourine while others began to clap. People were shouting Hallelujah, and some were even dancing in the aisle. The preacher got into the moment and jumped up and began to march up and down the bus spouting scripture and waving his bible over everyone's head. I even heard the bus driver shout, "Amen," over his shoulder. Skyla's tongue was keeping time with the music, and it was then I had a revelation!

I felt God was calling me into the ministry. The ministry of teaching French kissing to all the girls who had never known the real truth about God's divine plan for ultimate pleasure. I could see it now—I would be Frenching's pastor. In my mind, I could see the girls lining up in front of me during an invitation to give themselves to the one thing that would unlock the mysteries of what God truly wants us to understand. With this deeper revelation, we would be able to break the shackles of the *Thou shalt not's*. Segregated swimming by gender at church camp would no longer be needed.

I could see it all now—HALLELUJAH AND AMEN!

That last amen was an audible one into Skyla's mouth breaking the spell we were under. As she separated from me, she stared into my face, and I believe she understood this had been my first French kiss. Her smile was a mixture of 'Welcome to the world of Frenching' and 'You ain't seen nothin' yet.' Leaning back into my seat, I began to ponder what I had been missing in all those past relationships. I believed Skyla was truly heaven sent.

At that moment a meaty spit-wad smacked me on the left cheek. Ralph had taken advantage of the jubilation and stood looking over the seats to where I was sitting. His aim was perfect. I jumped up, headed straight toward him, and tripped over the pastor's wife's legs. The laughter broke my resolve to get even, and so I got up and turned back to my seat. I saw Skyla smiling, and it looked like she was partially sticking her tongue out at me through her teeth.

No, wait! It was my gum!

18

An Old, Brown Fedora

Sunrise has always drawn me to its warmth.

I'm from South Florida, and I can't stand being cold. It's cold here in Oklahoma even when it ain't. Too cold for this beach bum. Also, when the sun shines its morning light in the window, I can't just lie there—no matter what last night's consumptions involved. Usually, I awake from an all-night stone and quickly renew it so I won't have to face the day straight.

While the coffee is percolating, I roll a doobie and then, with a cup in hand, head for the front porch and my favorite rocking chair. That first inhale is held till the stone washes over my brain. I don't cough; my lungs don't spasm, because I am a seasoned stoner. I practice every day, and I must admit I'm at the Olympic level. I'd win a gold every time. In fact, I am usually smoking some Jamaican Gold just for training.

I always tip my head to the morning sun, thanking it for the day. That first warmth, that first buzz, that first sip makes the day possible.

I can do this!

As soon as the buzz and jolt settle in, I listen for the squeak of the rusty spring hinges on the torn wire-screen door from the ramshackle house next to me. And out he comes.

He's an old man—I'd guess in his eighties or more—bent over from all the years, almost Quasimodo-like except the hump stretches from shoulder to shoulder. He uses a cane to steady his bulk because, being bent over like that, his center of balance is off. His body is round from the chest up, which again has the effect of pulling him down and forward at the same time. But the off-center bulk does not rush his slow, tentative shuffle when he walks. His head is bald on top underneath the faded and dusty brown Fedora, but the hair on the sides is snow-like in color and in need of trimming. Nature's morning breeze blows it back ever so gently as if the wind herself had awakened just to comb his hair with her fingers. Even nature shows the deepest respect for this seasoned man.

His second-hand Walls department store pants are oversized and too long for his short legs, but he manages with the help of suspenders and a belt to keep the pant cuffs out from under black hand-polished shoes that are laced loosely and appear to have been tied with some degree of difficulty by hands that are swollen at the knuckles and curled from the years. The thumb on his right hand is bent backward from decades of licking and flipping pages in the "Good Book" as he puts it. His armpit-stained, white Oxford with a frayed collar and a missing button is covered by a wide, blue-and-red-striped tie. He wears a tie every day of the week, along with that old, brown Fedora.

Shuffling to the front edge of the porch he hangs his toes just over the lip but not enough to make his balance fragile. His head is down, watching each step carefully. Slowly he lifts his eyes and squints at the sun from under that hat. A smile spreads across his face, and he tilts his head backward to balance the offset bulk standing just over the edge, as he tips his hat and winks at Heaven.

And then the prayer begins.

It begins at full volume. He prays looking to heaven as if he is looking God right in the face. Shouts as if God is hard of hearing.

Almighty Father in Heaven above, I stand amazed in Your presence. I thank You for another day in which I may be your humbled servant and share Your Gospel with this lost and dying world . . .

And then he barely opens his right eye and turns his head ever so slightly so as to see that I am, indeed, listening to his next declaration.

. . . and for all those within my voice who are in need of Thy saving grace, I ask that Your Holy Spirit move them to repentance. Amen!

Then looking directly at me, he would lean his head back, and with a smile and a wink, he'd tip the edge of his old, brown Fedora and wish me a good morning.

Not today, old man—not today.

I came to this part of the country in '76 in my '67 split-windshield VW bus with my dog, Emmylou, and two months' worth of dope to hold me over until I made some connections or at least laid a crop in. I lived in the bus until I found work and was able to rent this shotgun house on South Lincoln. The old man was already a long-time fixture next door.

That first day, he hollered at me from his front porch that he would need a ride when his check came and would I oblige? Now I didn't know this old man, and it was not my nature to be sociable. I like to keep to myself and certainly was not wanting to make nice with a neighbor who might call the cops on me one day. But, Emmylou, she loves everyone. She immediately took it upon herself to go next door and meet this man who might be an avenue to treats. Emmylou is always on the lookout for treats or a pat for something well done.

I grunted some agreeance to the request, but quickly forgot it as I struggled with some furniture I had found at a *rag pullin'*—garage sale to folks here in Oklahoma—over on Broadway Avenue. The well-used, autumn-colored plaid couch was just twenty bucks, and they threw in the matching chair and ottoman for another five. Man, I was furniture rich!

Days later, while standing at the stove percolating coffee, I heard the front door open, followed by someone banging something against the living room walls. Emmylou got up barking and went to investigate. She stopped barking, and I assumed she was ok with the unannounced visitor. The banging continued into the bedroom, and before I could get turned around to see who was making all that racket, the old man was standing in my kitchen doorway banging the door jamb with his cane and hollering loud.

"Got my check! Check's in! Need you to carry me to the bank."

Emmylou stood behind him, wagging her approval. She was anxious to go for a ride.

"Man, watch that stick against my walls! And who the hell do you think you are just barging into a man's home demanding he take you to the bank? Man, it's only just seven-thirty in the morning. Banks don't open till nine."

My verbal challenge stopped the old man from coming into the kitchen. If he had swung that stick in the kitchen, he would have hit all the walls at once and done some real damage to me as well. The kitchen was too small for me to get out of his way, and the thought of being cane whipped before coffee and a toke just set me into a foul mood.

Resting his bulk with both hands on that cane, he looked up at me from under his old, brown Fedora and smiled with his eyes.

"I wear out walkin' to town. Sure could use a ride. Be glad to pay for your petrol."

He said that last line with some hesitancy, smiling that smile that disarmed me before my morning coffee and stone could.

And then from somewhere deep inside me came that part my mama instilled—that part that was gracious and kind to all. But it was only a part of that part.

"Go get in the bus. I'll be along directly."

Now the gracious part did intend to take the old man to his bank, but that other part—that mean part, that ornery part, that stone part—knew the old man, bent over as he was, could never get himself into the front seat of the bus.

That was the mean part.

I leaned over to the stove and lit my morning joint and took a big drag before heading out to see how the old man was progressing. I don't know if it was the stone or just my warped sense of humor, but when I got to the front door, I choked back a laugh that blew snot out of my nose.

The old man was frozen in position.

He had the left hand clutched to the seatback; he had the left leg bent and raised toward the bus step; he had the right-hand white-knuckling a grip on the door armrest, the cane swinging freely from his right wrist, all while balanced on the right leg which was shaking from all the weight. His face showed a determination that this was doable; however, his bulk and age would not allow him the flexibility to swing up into the seat.

It was then I realized my attempt at mean humor was about to backfire. The only way this man was getting into the front seat of the bus was if I lifted him up and in. Stepping back inside the living room, I took another hit and left the joint in the ashtray. Then looking at Emmylou to see if she agreed it was indeed a marvelous joke—she didn't—I stepped toward the old man and surveyed the situation. Just how was I going to get him into that seat without simple brute strength?

"You hang on to the seat back and the door rest while I pick you up and set you in. Think you can hang on?"

"I'll do my best. Don't cha have a lower car?"

Now I indeed did have a lower car — a yellow, black rag-top 1963 Austin Healy Sprite. But at the moment it was at a friend's house being worked on. Man, now wouldn't that be a sight, the three of us cruising around town in the Austin Healy—the old man with his hand holding on to his Fedora, Emmylou with her tongue hanging out licking the wind, and me with a shit-eating grin from my stone. Yessir, we would all be something to behold. However, getting the old man bent low enough to slide into the Sprite appeared to me just as difficult, if not more so, as getting him up and in the bus, so I let the idea go and did not tell him about my lower car.

My trade has made me fairly strong, but lifting dead weight into the high front seat of a VW bus takes more than I had anticipated. I knew that once I committed to the lift, I couldn't drop the man. No telling what might break on him and even worse he might land on me pinning me to the ground. I imagined lying there, both of us, for days. We lived on a dead-end street, and there was little to no traffic on it. I could send Emmylou for help, but somehow I figured she wouldn't be as successful as Lassie and would probably bring me her favorite bone instead of the phone.

I am convinced the three hernias I have are from that day. The exertion of lifting the old man must have pushed the stone right out of me, because I suddenly became soberly aware that this performance would have to be repeated at the bank. Little did I know at the time that the old man had many more stops in mind now that he had a ride.

Sure enough, after lifting him out of the bus and then back in when he finished his banking, he asked with that smile if I wouldn't mind taking him by the electric company, and then the gas company, and then the grocery store, and there was the post office, and finally the pharmacy. I told him he best get me some back-ache pills when he went into the pharmacy.

He didn't get the joke.

"Well, how about we swing by and get us a pizza before we head home?" I recommended from a post-stone munchie that needed satisfying.

Without looking at me, he replied, "Ain't never had no pizza before.

Always wanted to, just never did."

I looked at him with a surprise that didn't come from no stone. I had never met anyone who had never had pizza! I knew then it was my mission in life to lead this man to new pastures. I felt from somewhere deep inside that the greatest joy I would ever know was watching this old man take his first bite as pizza sauce ran down his chin and on to his wide tie.

We stopped at Mazzio's, and I asked the old man what he wanted on his pizza. Not only had he never eaten a pizza, but he had never given any thought as to what one might put on said pizza.

I suggested a supreme, and he could take off what he didn't like. Supreme, it was.

Back at his house, he invited me to share this meal at his table. The house was dimly lit, dusty, and cluttered with years and years of magazines and newspapers and books. The books looked mostly to be Bibles. I made a joke and asked if he was a Bible salesman in his working days.

"Well, sorta. I was a tent-revival travelin' preacher," and then he smiled that smile.

Holy crap! I thought silently with creased eyebrows and a tight-lipped frown.

Now it all makes sense. The loud morning prayer, the ties, the Bibles. I was living next door to a Bible thumper and not just any ol' Bible thumper, but one who seemed to be on a mission to drag this long-hair with him when he started heavenward. I imagined him clutching my hand and holding on as he flew up to meet Jesus. I imagined him giving me the option to believe, or he would let go as we climbed higher and higher. I looked down at Emmylou to see what her reaction was to this new information, and she looked up at me with a look that suggested my days as a stoner were numbered. She also wondered if any pizza bones were coming her way?

Hoping to get him on to something else other than my personal eternal damnation, I asked, "So, did you have your own tent and travel around in a bus? Bet you were one of those fire and brimstone preachers—right? Get 'em saved and dunk them in a horse trough before they can change their mind. Am I right?"

He didn't get the back-ache joke earlier, so this attempt at humor was even less successful. But I tried again hoping he would think about anything but saving my wretched soul.

Smiling as he handed me a paper plate, a paper towel, and a plastic fork, he spoke softly and with fondness in his voice, "Yes, I had a tent. It was a big blue-and-white-striped tent that could seat up to 500 folks at one time. I had a big moving van that hauled the tent and the chairs and a pulpit. My wife drove the pick-up camper, and I followed in the moving van. I had a sign painter paint in big red letters on the side of the van—Jesus Saves. Folks could see us a-comin' for miles."

Surprised, I looked up smiling and said, "You was married?"

Sitting down slowly, he looked off to the small-framed picture on his mantle and whispered, "I was married to the most beautiful girl in all of Oklahoma. Her name was Bernice. I called her Buddy."

Then turning toward me, he winked and leaned close as he smiled, "She was my best friend, so I called her my Buddy."

I could see the tears of memories forming around the corners of his eyes. Then sitting back in his chair, he bowed his head and said grace over the pizza and thanked the Lord for his new friend and he prayed for my salvation.

He made no attempt for the rest of the evening to save my soul. Emmylou got a bag full of pizza bones to take home.

Several days later, I heard a car door open and slam. Not expecting anyone, I looked out the front screen door and saw a polished, older model Lincoln Continental parked out front of the old man's house. I could hear the voices of the old man and a woman inside. The woman seemed insistent about something the old man didn't agree with. I never heard the old man raise his voice in anger, but it was certain he didn't want to do whatever it was she proposed.

The squeaky screen door opened and a thin woman dressed in a below the knee-length skirt with a matching jacket and modest heels, who appeared to be in her late 40s or more, stepped out. From the flush in her cheeks, I could tell she was not happy. She put some folded papers in her purse as she pulled out her keys and then noticed she was being observed.

She spoke without looking up, "Good morning. Looks to be a nice day ahead of us, don't cha think?"

Then stepping to the end of the porch, she introduced herself.

"My name is Reverend Alice Franklin. I pastor the church over on south Oak Avenue, the First Pentecostal Holiness Church of God. You should come visit us sometime. We'd love to have you."

Opening my screen door, me and Emmylou stepped out onto the porch. Emmylou normally wags her tail at someone she meets for the first time, but she just laid down on the porch, and I swear I heard her growl.

"Morning. Name's MJ. You a friend of the old man?"

"I'm his pastor. We always come by on Sunday morning in the church van and pick him up. We could pick you up as well. What do you say?"

Her offer of a ride on Sunday was given over her shoulder as she turned to her car. Opening the driver's side door, she looked back toward me with eyes that felt more cold than inviting. She asked again, "May we expect you?"

I mumbled a 'never know' reply and watched as she drove off. After she drove out of sight, Emmylou and I immediately headed next door. I found the old man sitting at his kitchen table looking down at what appeared to be legal papers. He didn't seem to notice me at first until

Emmylou went over and licked his hand.

Looking up with a weak smile, he offered, "What can I do for you, neighbor?"

"Just makin' sure you're ok."

Handing me the papers he said without looking up, "They want to put me in a nursing home. I don't wanna go. I like livin' here by myself. Besides, I got you and Emmylou next door if'n I need anything." Then tilting his head and smiling genuinely, he winked at me. He reached down and gave Emmylou a gentle pat on the head while she wagged her tail and laid down next to him.

After studying the papers quickly and handing them back, I asked, "Can they make you?"

"These papers seem to indicate that at some time, I gave the preacher a power of attorney. I don't remember doin' that, but this here is my signature," he said as he looked down again at the papers and tapped the line with what appeared to be his name.

Then looking back up with tears in his eyes, he whispered, "I really don't wanna go."

"You ain't goin' nowhere! Not as long as I'm here. Look, I got to run back home to Florida for a couple of weeks, but I'll be back, and when I get back, we'll get them papers changed. Promise me you won't go nowhere or do nuthin' till I get back. And don't sign nuthin', ya here."

He smiled faintly at me and gave Emmylou another gentle pat on the head, then smiled again at me and nodded his head.

Eleven days later, the old man was dead.

It seems that while I was away, the lady preacher swooped in and had the old man moved into a nursing home. She declared he was unable to care for himself and as his legal guardian, she was doing what she thought was best for his personal safety. He died alone one night in his sleep.

When I got back to Oklahoma, a friend informed me of what

happened, and I immediately went next door to see that it was true. Emmylou ran ahead not knowing what had happened.

The house was quiet and empty. His furniture was gone, and so were all the magazines and Bibles. The place had been swept clean of the dust. Almost as if they expected to move someone else in soon. Then something caught my eye, and I knew in a moment this had not been the old man's idea.

The picture of his "Buddy" was still on the mantle along with an old brown Fedora.

Several mornings later while sitting quietly in the morning sun with my coffee and joint, I decided that I would go visit the old man at the local cemetery and take him his picture of his wife.

Emmylou wanted to come along.

Along the route to the cemetery, I noticed a pasture off to my left and in the middle of the pasture was what looked like a circus tent. It was blue with white stripes.

A sign out front read—Jesus Saves—in big red letters.

Oh, what the hell. This is for you old man.

I told Emmylou to wait and promised I'd be right back. She wasn't so certain.

The meetin', as they called it, was under full swing. They were singing and banging tambourines. Some man up front seemed to be in charge. He was encouraging the crowd to sit down and come to order. He began to toss out the fire and brimstone. Folks were shouting "Amen" and slapping those tambourines. Some even jumped up now and then to shout a "Hallelujah!"

Several of them started looking real hard at me.

I thought of the old man just then and how he never judged me, but just seemed to enjoy my company. He never said a word about the length of my hair or the fact that I smoked a lot of pot. He never complained about me toting him around in the VW bus. He seemed to truly enjoy the pizzas we shared. He called me his friend and neighbor.

When the crowd stood again, I slipped out the back of the tent and into the cool night air. The stars were brilliantly shining down. I imagined the old man looking down on me, standing upright and not all bent over. He no longer needed his cane. He still had on that old brown Fedora and smiled that smile. I realized at that moment how much I was going to miss him.

So I thought when I headed to the front porch in the morning, along with just my coffee, I'd start my day with looking God right in the eye and shouting how amazing the day is. And just to make sure the old man heard me, too, I'd lean my head back and with a smile and a wink, I'd tip the edge of an old, brown Fedora.

Acknowledgments

Let me begin by saying that this work would not have happened without the various people mentioned below. There is no particular order, nor is there a hierarchy intended within the people mentioned, and it is quite likely I've left someone off the list—though not intentional. But I would have to say that there are several key people who are responsible for getting this project off the ground. Julie Chappell and Hank Jones, my dear friends, started this. They invited me along to their various poet conferences and unleashed the prose within. A prose man amongst a bunch of poets. Somehow, I found my place. What a delightful world of creative writers to be included in. More than you will ever know, I am forever grateful to you both for starting this. Thank you, Julie and Hank.

Every writer needs at least one who enjoys his/her work. I am very fortunate to have many who have always encouraged me to keep writing, in particular, Mallory Young, who let me try out the stories on her first and then on her students.

To Mike Pierce, a man whom I greatly admire and consider a friend. I have never known a man who has read as much as you. And yet you always found time to read these silly tales of mine.

Yvonne Mulhern, thanks for being interested enough to ask if there were any new stories for you to read.

If I only had you three to write for, I would be content because you make me feel like my simple contribution is worthy.

Ken Hada, the rock star of creative writing festivals, once asked me,

"When you going to have a book on the book table?" Well, here it is, Ken. Thanks for believing in me. And thanks for that late-night text that got me connected to my publisher.

Jeanelle Barrett, you too, share in this reality. You set for me a deadline to produce this work. Thanks, boss.

Again, thanks to Julie, Hank, and Paul Juhasz for their wonderful editing skills. And thanks, Hank, for the monster poem to open this work.

To my son, Daniel who laughed at my stupid stories over the years (don't let your daughter, Kyndall read this until she's old enough. Don't want to ruin her view of Poppa. By the way, I hope I didn't ruin your view of Dad.).

To my lovely bride of 38+ years, Kelli, I thank you for letting Woodstok exist, and I'll keep my promise not to let him come home and live with us.

To my sister, Elaine, thanks for enjoying these tales (so glad I found you).

To my other sister, Debbie, you are in the story of the tourists and the gator, but to protect you, I changed the name and the gender. Oh, crap! I just took away your protection. Sorry, Sis.

And to you, Pop who gave me the gift of storytelling—miss you still.

Finally, to Terry and Roxie Kirk, my publishers at Fine Dog Press. It all started with that late-night text from Ken when he said to me, "I think you two would make a great fit." He was right. Roxie, you were and are forever the encourager. Your excitement became mine. Thank you.

About the Author

Woodstok Farley began his life in the southeast corner of the U.S. close to the coastline on the edge of a swamp. He traveled the U.S. in a VW beetle furthering his education of this fascinating country. After settling in Texas, Woodstok found himself more comfortable in sandals than boots and began to write about his yearning to return to the seacoast through the characters in his many tales. Those yearnings have been collected in his debut book entitled *As the Wave Rose: Florida Tales and Other Wandering Stories* published by Fine Dog Press.

www.ingramcontent.com/pod-product-compliance
Lightning Source LLC
Chambersburg PA
CBHW030745110726
47900CB00008B/2466